The Delaware Detectives:

Through

Many

Dangers

Dana Rongione

The Delaware Detectives:

Through Many Dangers

Book 2

The Delaware Detectives

Mystery Series

Published by

A Word Fitly Spoken Press

Text copyright © Dana Rongione, 2014

Illustrations copyright © Vineet Siddhartha, 2014

ISBN-13: 978-1497485600
ISBN-10: 1497485606

Table of Contents

Books by Dana Rongione

The Delaware Detectives Mystery Series:

Book #1 – The Delaware Detectives: A Middle-Grade Mystery

Book #2 – Through Many Dangers

Books for Young Children:

Through the Eyes of a Child

God Can Use My Differences

Books for Adults:

Random Ramblings of a Raving Redhead

There's a Verse for That

'Paws'itively Divine: Devotions for Dog Lovers

The Deadly Darts of the Devil

Improve Your Health Naturally

Creating a World of Your Own: Your Guide to Writing Fiction

Audio:

Moodswing Mania – a study through select Psalms

There's a Verse for That – Scripture with a soft music background

Excerpt from Book 1
in the Series

I studied the rows of faces looking back at me —George Washington, Abraham Lincoln, Benjamin Franklin. I studied the color of each stamp, from eerie yellows to rosy reds. "Okay, I don't get it. What am I looking for?"

Jamie gave another sigh. "Do I have to do everything? Look at the dates."

I turned my attention back to the page and gasped in excitement. "They're in chronological order!"

"Chrono-what?" Jamie asked.

"Chronological order. It means in order of the dates. See." I pointed at the first stamp on the page and moved my finger across the page. This first one here was made in 1881, and this next one, 1882, then 1883, and so on. All we have to do is put the stamps in order by the year they were made, and we'll have the first part of the message."

"I know that," Jamie snapped. "I'm the one who told you they were in order. Remember?"

"It doesn't really matter. The important thing is that now we can read the message."

As we sorted through the stamps, I could not believe I had overlooked something so simple. How embarrassing to be outsmarted by my little brother! Luckily, no one else was there to see, but that didn't keep him from smiling that ridiculous *I'm-so-smart* smile.

After several minutes, we had the first page of stamps in order. We turned them over so that we could see the writing on the back of each stamp and stared at the message that was spread before us. "The secret may be found where the water goes round and round," I read aloud.

"Yes!" Jamie shouted. "I knew it. It *is* about a secret treasure! I told you so!"

"We don't know that," I said, but I was beginning to wonder if he might be right. Could this be a clue to a hidden fortune? If so, what in the world did it mean?

Are you ready for a treasure hunt?

Pick up Book 1 in the Delaware Detectives Mystery Series.

Acknowledgments

This book would not have been possible without help from the following people:

My sweet husband, Jason – You are such an inspiration to me and often give me the "kick in the pants" I need to keep writing. Thank you for your love, constructive criticism and that strong shoulder on which I often cry. You are the love of my life, and I'm a better person because of you.

Tara and Aaron – Thank you for reading this book and giving me some valuable insights on how to make it better. I know you spent a lot of time and effort to work with me on making this book even better than the first. Words cannot describe how grateful I am for that. You are both a blessing!

Tamatha – When I asked you to read my book, I had no idea of the health problems you were about to face. Still, you soldiered on and, despite your own circumstances, took the time to read the book and provide helpful feedback. You brought to light some things that I had never thought about and had me wondering, *How do you know this stuff?* Thank you for being such a loyal friend.

Abby – Thank you for volunteering to be a beta reader as well as the model for my main character. When I wrote this book, I needed only to think of you, and the words, actions and expressions of the character would come bursting forth. You are an inspiration to me, and you have been a help in more ways than you can possibly know.

Jason (from Save the Valley) – I can't tell you the number of people I contacted for the information I needed to make this book as accurate as possible. Most of them ignored my requests, but you didn't. You went above and beyond by providing me with information, pictures, maps and much more. This book could not have happened without you. Thank you for taking the time to help me. You're a blessing!

Mom and Dad, Lanie, Dawn, Toni, Nancy, Jerry and Sophia, Julien, Walter and Sharon, Qun Shi, Shelley, Ashley and anonymous contributors – Your financial support during my fundraising campaign was an invaluable part of bringing this book to life. I simply could not have gotten to this point without your generous donations of money, love and prayers. May God richly bless each of you for your thoughtfulness.

Vineet – You did a wonderful job on the illustrations and added new depth to the story. Thank you for taking the time and effort to work with me in order to get each picture just as I imagined.

Lisa – Your editing services were a Godsend. Thank you for working me into your busy schedule and giving my book the final polishing it needed. I have enjoyed getting to know you better through the John 3:16 Marketing Network and hope that we will continue to grow closer in the Lord.

A Quick Note to the Reader

While the main goal of this book is your enjoyment, there are several added features that will hopefully increase your knowledge and help you to appreciate the joy of learning. Among these features is a glossary of terms. As you read through the story, you will notice certain words that are marked by a small number. In the back of the book, you'll find the glossary that contains the number, the word associated with that number and the definition of the word. So, if at any time you don't understand one of the marked words, know that you can flip to the glossary and uncover its meaning.

The book also contains a science center which details an easy experiment you can try at home. This experiment is the same one Abby and Jamie perform in this book, so you can try it out and judge the results for yourself.

Lastly, there is a section called, "History Hideout," that provides information about some of the historical facts mentioned in this book and resources that can offer even more insight. I will tell you this: if you're interested in reading the next book in the series, you may want to brush up on some of the history mentioned in the hideout. It may be the key to solving the next mystery.

For now, let's begin the hunt!

Prologue

With every breath, the man struggled to make sense of his surroundings. In the blackness that engulfed him, he strained his ears to pick out a sound, any sound that signified that help was on its way. The pain in both his left leg and arm was blinding, so he did his best to think on better things. Surely a rescue had already been set in motion. The only problem was that nobody knew his location. And if he was honest, the likelihood of anyone figuring it out was slim. In frustration, he leaned his head against the wall and closed his eyes as a single tear rolled down his cheek, its fall to the floor drowned out by the steady trickle of water nearby. Drip, Drip, Drip!

Chapter One:
Making a List
and Checking It Twice

"Why did you tell that little girl we'd find her dad?" Jamie asked as he paced up and down within the confines of the narrow room.

"Because I thought we could," I answered. "And that little girl has a name. It's Maria, and she's not that little. She's the same age as you are."

Jamie flopped into the black bean bag in the corner. "I know," he huffed. "But it's been three days now, and we've not found a single clue. Not a hair. Not a piece of cloth. Not a footprint. Nothing. It's like the guy just vanished."

I stared at the empty bulletin board—the one Pop-Pop had hung for us so we could have a place to accumulate all the clues. Unfortunately, Jamie was right. There wasn't a single clue. If Maria's father was still alive, he was probably in some sort of trouble. But what kind, who knew?

Mr. Baker had been missing for two weeks before Maria sought us out. She had seen the headlines in the newspaper where we had solved a mystery concerning a hidden fortune, and even though the police were already on the case, she had asked for our help. I guess I had been feeling a little sure of myself after solving our first mystery, but as I stared at the empty clue board, I was beginning to think we probably should have left this case to the professionals.

Shaking my head to expel such negative thoughts, I swiveled my chair back around to face my brother. "Let's go over the facts one more time. Maybe we've missed something."

"Abby," Jamie whined. "We've been over the facts a million times. There's nothing there. No hint as to where this man is."

"Still," I said, trying to maintain my patience, "we should review what we know. Sometimes that's the key to solving the mystery. We just need to look harder. Let's take a few minutes and rehearse what we know, making sure we don't leave anything out. All right?"

Jamie struggled to his feet. "Fine, but if we're going to go through the whole thing again, let's write each fact down on an index card or something and pin it to the board. I'm tired of looking at all that empty space!"

"Deal," I said, pulling open the desk drawer and rummaging around for some index cards and a pen. With the cards before me and pen in hand, I began recalling the events leading up to the disappearance of Maria's father. "First off, we know that Mr. Baker works as a trail steward and that he left his home on Thursday, June nineteenth to fulfill his trail duties for the day." I scribbled the notes as quickly as possible while making sure they were still neat enough for me to be able to read later.

Before I had finished writing, Jamie chimed in. "We also know that he never returned home that evening. In fact, no one he worked with on the trail system remembered seeing him at all that day."

"Yes," I interrupted, "but that doesn't mean anything. His coworkers also said that he often worked alone, preferring the quiet of the woods to the chatter of fellow workers. It's possible he could have gone out on the trail before anyone else arrived. After all, there are a lot of trails out there, and his job is to walk the trails to check the condition of the paths, as well as to help other trail users with directions and such." I stretched and flexed my fingers that were beginning to cramp from trying to write so fast. "Here," I shoved the cards and pen toward Jamie. "You write for a while."

I rose from my chair and scooted past Jamie as he made his way to the desk. As soon as his bottom hit the seat, he began writing.

"Did you think of something else?" I asked, rubbing my index finger along the bookshelves that had already begun to gather dust.

"Just that the police and other trail workers have already searched up and down the trails and found no trace of Mr. Baker."

"Right," I sighed. "I even talked with the officer in charge, and it seems like they're in the same situation we're in. There's nothing to indicate that anything has happened to Mr. Baker except for the fact that he never came home. At this point, the police are suggesting that perhaps he simply left of his own free will."

Jamie slammed the pen down on the desk top. "But what kind of man would leave his daughter? What kind of man would just walk away from his family? Maria's already lost her mom. Surely, he wouldn't leave her too. Would he?" Retracing my steps, I looked into my brother's eyes. "I don't know, Jamie. I don't know anything about Mr. Baker, but from what Maria's told us, I don't think he would leave her. I think he's a loving father and that something has happened to him. It's up to us to find out what!"

"But that's all we know," Jamie complained. "Look." He held up the cards. "We don't even know enough information to fill up a handful of cards. This is hopeless, Abby."

With my fists balled, I stomped over to the chair and stood in the most menacing position I could muster. "No, it's not hopeless. You're forgetting what the Bible says. Over and over again in the New Testament, God tells us that the things that are impossible with men are possible with God. Is God on our side or not?"

Jamie lowered his gaze to the floor. "Well, yeah, I guess."

"Then we'll find Mr. Baker. Don't you think God wants us to find him? Don't you think He wants Maria to be with her dad again?"

"Sure," Jamie said, meeting my gaze once again. "But how are we going to find him?"

"I don't know," I confided. "But I know we will. We can't give up, okay?"

Jamie nodded and began pinning the index cards on the bulletin board. "But can we take a break now? I'm hungry."

I laughed. "Now there's a shock! Come on. We'll go get some lunch."

We flipped off the lights and left the room that Pop-Pop had helped us set up as our office. After solving our first mystery and being asked to work on a second, Pop-Pop (that's what we call our grandfather) determined that we ought to have a place for our detective work. He offered us the room at the bottom of the steps. It's not a big room, but it's enough to suit our needs.

Pop-Pop did all the hard work, like moving in the furniture which included a nice desk, an office chair and a couple of narrow bookshelves. He also hung the bulletin board behind the desk. Jamie and I got to add the final touches like the giant bean bag and the light-blocking curtains so that we could work without fear of someone looking in. The curtains also helped to keep the room cooler and darker, which kind of made it feel like a small cave.

Jamie and I actually live in South Carolina, which is more than six hundred miles away from here, but since we don't get to visit our family in Delaware very often, our parents thought it would be a good idea for us kids to spend the summer with our grandfather. At first, Jamie and I were afraid that we would be bored out of our minds, but I must admit that the summer had not turned out exactly as we had thought it would. In fact, it had been one adventure after another.

"I wish Scott and Phyllis were here," Jamie said as he opened the refrigerator door and stared into its depths.

"Yeah, me too."

Scott and Phyllis were neighbors of Pop-Pop's. We only met them a few weeks ago, but in that time, we had really grown close. Phyllis was about Jamie's age and, believe it or not, acted a lot like Jamie. I wouldn't say she was a tomboy, but neither was she a girly girl. And as for Scott, well, let's just say he was a very nice young man that I wouldn't mind getting to spend more time with.

Unfortunately, the siblings were on their yearly summer vacation to Disney World. Yes, you read that right. They went to Disney World every summer. I've never even been to Disney World. I can't imagine getting to go every summer. But that's where they went, leaving Jamie and me here alone to solve this tangle of all tangles. Even Pop-Pop hadn't been much help in the case because of the increase in business down at the store. Funny, for someone who was retired, he sure spent a lot of time at work. I guess that's just the way he was raised. He was taught to work hard and to help whenever he could. On top of that, there was recently an accident where another manager was injured and had to have surgery. Since he was going to be out of work for several weeks, Pop-Pop was filling in for him at the store, which meant Jamie and I were doing our best to help out around the house and take care of ourselves while Pop-Pop was away. It wasn't the perfect way to spend the summer, but we certainly had enough to keep us busy. Besides, we were used to being on our own since our parents were both at work a lot too.

Not finding what he was looking for in the refrigerator, Jamie closed the door, opened up the pantry, and pushed aside cans and boxes on the middle shelf. "Ah, now we're talking," he declared, pulling out a giant box of instant macaroni and cheese. "Can you fix this?" he asked, scanning the back of the package.

Rolling my eyes, I replied, "Yes, but what do you want to go with it?"

"With it?" he asked. "Why do I need anything with it? Macaroni and cheese can stand on its own. It's a complete meal in my book."

With a shake of my head, I took the box from his hand and opened the bottom cabinet door to find a saucepan. For the next few minutes, I prepared our "complete meal" while Jamie grabbed forks, napkins and bowls. Within minutes, we were sitting down at the table.

"Wait!" I said to Jamie who was holding a forkful of macaroni and cheese just inches from his mouth. "We need to say grace."

"Oh, right," he said, dropping his fork to his bowl with a loud clank. "Go ahead."

I bowed my head and closed my eyes. "Dear Lord, thank you for this food and for this day. Please help us to find Maria's dad. We know he's out there somewhere, Lord, and we know that you know where he is. Please give us a clue. Help us, Lord. In Jesus' name, amen."

We spent the rest of the day playing board games and straightening the house, all in an effort to take our minds off the mystery at hand. We both knew how important it was to find Maria's dad, but we also knew that we had nothing to go on. And that knowledge was discouraging beyond belief. Our next step was a blur. We had no idea where to even begin looking.

And so, we did nothing.

As I climbed into bed that night, my thoughts were a whirlwind of ideas about how to help Pop-Pop around the house and how to help Maria find her father. The more I tried to settle my thoughts, the more they seemed to press on me. I felt sad and discouraged, and I wasn't really sure why. Suddenly, I noticed the rain pitter-pattering against the metal roof. The sound was soothing, like a wordless song, but the tapping rhythm quickly turned into a driving beat. The sound of rolling thunder blended with the clanking of the pouring rain. Lightning flashed across the sky, illuminating[1] the entire room.

This was the second severe storm we had experienced since coming to stay with Pop-Pop. The first one had nearly scared me to death, but this time, though the storm seemed just as violent, it wasn't the main cause of my concern. As the lightning flashed once again across the sky, a thought flashed across my mind.

It was gone just as quickly as it came, but in that moment, I realized it was just the lead we had been looking for.

Chapter Two:
Doggone It!

When I awoke the next morning, I noticed the rain had stopped. Unfortunately, my spinning thoughts had not, which probably explained why I felt so tired and sluggish. It's hard to sleep with so many ideas clattering around in your brain.

Despite my foggy thinking, I was eager to get up and start the day. After three days of having absolutely no idea where to begin to look for Maria's father, hope had arrived . . . finally. I don't know why we hadn't thought of it before, but I was determined not to waste any more time thinking about it. It was time for action.

After dressing, I strode into Jamie's room and began shaking him. "Wake up, Jamie. We have a mystery to solve."

He only moaned and jerked the covers up over his head.

"Oh, no you don't!" I declared, pulling his covers down to his feet. "Get up. I have an idea. I think I might know where to look for Maria's father."

That got his attention. He jumped out of the bed and began rummaging[2] through his drawers. "Well, why didn't you say so? Where do you wanna look? Where do you think he is?"

I looked down at my watch. Eight thirty. Pop-Pop didn't need to leave until nine o'clock, so maybe he would have time to take us for a short ride.

"I'll tell you all about it in a minute. Why don't you get dressed while I go talk to Pop-Pop? Then I'll tell you everything."

Jamie growled but did as I asked.

I made my way down the stairs, noticing the skip in my step that had been absent the past few days.

It's amazing what a difference a little hope makes in a person's outlook and attitude.

Walking from room to room, I searched for Pop-Pop, calling out his name as I went. When I didn't find him, I hurried back to the kitchen and looked on the table. Sure enough, there was a small note addressed to us. My happiness fled, and a knot formed in the pit of my stomach. I knew what the note meant. Pop-Pop was not here. So much for my plan!

When Jamie finally arrived downstairs, I was sitting at the table holding the note. Tears of frustration coursed down my cheeks. Try as I might, I simply could not contain my disappointment.

"What's wrong?" Jamie asked.

"Pop-Pop had to leave early," I replied flatly. "Evidently that's part of his responsibilities for the next little while. He has to be there before the store opens." I threw the card down on the table. "I guess he forgot to tell us that part."

Jamie looked into my eyes, obviously uncertain about my strange mood. "Well, Abby, he was pretty upset about Phillip getting hurt and everything. So, he forgot to tell us one little thing. It's no big deal."

Blowing out a deep breath, I nodded. "You're right. I'm not upset at Pop-Pop. It's just that I was really hoping he could give us a ride somewhere this morning, but now, we'll have to wait until tonight or maybe even tomorrow."

Jamie sat down across from me. "Does this have anything to do with the mystery?"

Again, I nodded.

After a moment of silence, Jamie raised his eyebrows. "Well, are you going to tell me, or do I have to try to guess?"

"Yeah, I'll tell you, but let's get some breakfast. I'll tell you while we eat. Deal?"

"Deal," Jamie said.

For the next few minutes, we prepared our meal. It wasn't exactly the breakfast of champions, but in my book, there's nothing wrong with cereal or toaster pastries. They're quick and easy, and best of all, they don't make much mess. I guess I've realized the importance of that now that I'm the one who has to clean up.

For a few moments, the only sounds in the big house were the clanking of my spoon against my cereal bowl and the smacking of Jamie's lips as he devoured his pastries. Unable to contain my new hunch any longer, I finally spilled out the thoughts that had haunted me in the night.

"The storm last night gave me a great idea."

"There was a storm last night?" Jamie interrupted. "I didn't hear anything."

"That's because you sleep like the dead," I commented. "But that's not the point. Remember a few weeks ago, right after we got here, when we had that really bad storm?"

Jamie nodded as he set his glass of milk down on the table. "Yeah, it was scary. I definitely didn't sleep through that one."

"Right. Well, I was thinking that *that* storm took place right about the same time that Maria's dad went missing."

I paused to sec if Jamie had put the pieces together yet, but he only looked at me as if waiting for me to continue.

"What if Maria's dad went to work that day and was out on one of the trails when the storm hit?"

Jamie wiped his mouth and shook his head. "But the police and rangers and the other trail people— or whatever they're called—have already checked the trails. There wasn't any sign of him. Remember?"

"Right," I agreed, "but they checked the trails. What if he left the trail to find shelter from the storm? Remember, hiking out here isn't like hiking at home. There are no mountains or caves or outcroppings along the trail. If someone wanted to find shelter, he'd have to find it elsewhere, like an old cabin or mine or something like that."

Jamie sat quietly for a moment. From the look on his face, he was pondering what I had just told him. Suddenly, he looked up. "But don't you think the police would have thought of that? I mean, it's their job. Don't you think they would have thought to look around the trails for places he could have gone?"

For the second time in one morning, my hopes were dashed. I hadn't thought about the fact that the police may have already searched the surrounding areas for signs that Mr. Baker had taken refuge to wait out the storm. Since the idea had just come to me, I guess I thought I was the only one who had come up with the possibility. But Jamie was right. The police were professionals. They knew how to do their jobs. They had probably searched the area and even spoken to people who lived around there to find out if anyone had seen him. And they still had no leads to go on.

Who was I to think that I could solve this mystery when they couldn't?

Once again, Jamie's voice dragged me from my thoughts. "It was a good idea, Abby. A really good idea. Even if the police already checked out the area, it wouldn't hurt to look again, right?"

"Yeah," I mumbled. "I guess we could look. I don't know what else to do."

"It's okay, Abby. We'll find him. I know we will."

I looked up at my little brother and realized for the first time just how much he had grown. "You know, we've changed since we've gotten here. Remember how we used to fight?"

Jamie smiled. "How could I forget? I guess there's something about solving a mystery that makes you grow up a little. Maybe it's all that teamwork stuff."

Returning his smile, I said, "Yeah, maybe so." I rose from the table and picked up my bowl, spoon and empty glass. "Why don't we go ahead and get some of this mess cleaned up, and then we can figure out what to do with the day since we won't be going out to look for Mr. Baker."

"Why can't we go look for him?" Jamie asked, joining me at the sink.

"Because Maria lives a couple of towns over and the trails that Mr. Baker works on are a couple of towns over from that. It's too far to walk. That's why I was hoping to catch Pop-Pop before he left."

"Oh," Jamie muttered. "I see."

As I worked on the dishes from breakfast and gathered up the laundry, Jamie walked from room to room collecting the trash into one large trash bag to take to the outside trash can. He had only been outside for a few minutes when his holler echoed through the house.

"Abby, come here!"

Afraid that he was hurt or in danger, I threw down the basket of clothes and ran out to meet him. He was kneeling on the ground beside the trash can, staring into the dark space between the can and the house.

"What is it, Jamie? You scared me half to death."

"It's a puppy," Jamie replied. "I think he's scared of me. He won't come out."

Kneeling beside my brother, I saw that there was indeed a puppy—albeit a large puppy—cowering in the darkness. His face was mostly brown, though the section around his nose was white and led to a thin stripe that made its way between his eyes and up to his forehead. He seemed to have two small black patches just below his ears, but that could have just been shadows. From the way he was turned, I couldn't really see his body, but I couldn't miss his eyes. They were deep brown and looked so very sad.

Reaching out my hand in a low, palm-up position, I cooed[3] to the poor pup. "It's okay, cutie. We won't hurt you. Come on out of there."

The dog only whimpered and pressed himself further back into the cubby hole. Whether or not he was a stray I couldn't even begin to guess, but one thing that was certain was that he was terrified.

"We need to find a way to get him out of there without scaring him even more," I told Jamie.

"I know, but how?"

I looked around, then formulated[4] a plan. "I'm going to pull the trash can out nice and slow. You stay there and keep the dog's attention. Maybe once the trash can is out of the way, he won't feel so trapped, and we'll be able to get to him."

"Do you think it will work?" Jamie asked.

"I'm not sure, but I don't have a better idea. Do you?"

Jamie shook his head, then looked back at the dog. As he spoke to the pup in a calm voice, I carefully slid the trash can straight out away from the house, opening up the space in which the dog sat. If the dog noticed the movement, he didn't react.

Once the can was a good two feet away from the house, I knelt beside Jamie again. Without the shadow from the trash can, I could make out the rest of the dog's features. In contrast to his brown head, his body was a spotted combination of black and white. There didn't seem to be any brown on his body at all. I had never seen a dog like it. It was almost like someone had taken the head from one dog and the body from another dog and spliced them together. He was adorable, but definitely unique.

As we watched, the pup shifted his weight and began inching forward. He took two steps then pulled his head back as if he was afraid we were going to grab him. To be honest, I had thought about it, but after noticing this reaction, I decided to just wait for him to come to us.

I don't know how long we remained there in the dirt, but the anxious dog finally crept from his hiding place and stood before us. After a few initial sniffs, he licked the hand that rested in my lap, but as soon as I moved to pet him, he jumped back.

"He sure is a scaredy cat, I mean, dog," Jamie snickered. "Get it, a scaredy dog."

Unimpressed with his humor, I chose not to respond. Instead, I carefully slid my hand down to the ground right in front of the dog. He approached it cautiously, sniffed, then began licking again. As he licked, I bent my fingers so that they gently caressed his chin. At first, he flinched, but before long, he leaned into my hand, eager for the attention.

"Do you think he's a stray?" Jamie asked.

I pointed to the worn blue collar. "I don't know. He has a collar, but I don't see any tags. And he's awfully thin. If he's not a stray, then his owners don't seem to be taking very good care of him."

"Let's keep him!" Jamie exclaimed, leaping up from the ground, causing the pup to jump back in fear.

"Careful, Jamie. You scared him. You can't jump around like that. Not right now, anyway. As for keeping him, aren't you forgetting a few things?"

"Like what?" Jamie asked.

"Well, like the fact that we don't know if he's a stray or the fact that we don't know what Pop-Pop would say about taking on another mouth to feed or the fact that we live hundreds of miles from here."

"Oh, that." Jamie hung his head, and I immediately regretted my harsh tone.

"I'm sorry, Jamie. It's just that taking in a dog is a lot of responsibility, and I'm not sure we're in a place to handle that right now. Do you understand?"

"Yeah, you're right," he mumbled as he scraped his foot along the dirt. "So what do we do with him?"

I looked down at the bundle of fur that had nearly fallen asleep in my lap. As much as I wanted to keep him, I knew we had to do the right thing for everyone.

"I guess the first step is to find out if he has an owner," I told Jamie.

"But how do we do that?"

How indeed? It looked like we now had two mysteries to solve. Good grief!

Chapter Three:

Detectives or Dogwalkers?

After some thought, Jamie and I decided to give the dog some milk then make a call to the local animal shelter. Surely, if someone lost a dog, one of the first places he would call would be the shelter, right? Well, we were about to find out.

I made the call while Jamie sat on the back porch with the poor dog that was devouring the bowl of milk like he hadn't eaten in months. We had debated over bringing him inside, but I just didn't feel right allowing a dog to come in without Pop-Pop's permission, so we agreed he'd have to stay outside until we figured out what to do with him.

After talking with the kind lady at the shelter, I hung up the phone and went out to meet Jamie.

"What did they say?" he asked before I'd even gotten through the doorway.

"The lady said that no one had called in a description of a dog like that. In fact, she said that they hadn't had any reports of a missing dog in the past couple of weeks."

A gentle pressure against my foot caused me to look down. The puppy had left his empty bowl and was now chewing on my shoe.

"No, don't do that," I scolded, gently tapping the end of his nose.

He looked up at me, then resumed his chewing. Deciding that he was too big to pick up, I squatted beside him, hoping that some loving attention would distract him from my shoes. Once I was down on his level, the dog nuzzled against me, leaning hard into my leg and allowing his back end to slide to the ground.

Jamie giggled. "He's a mess!"

"He sure is," I agreed, "but he's a cute mess." I rubbed the soft head as it pressed more firmly into my leg, like the pup couldn't seem to get close enough.

Jamie walked over to the railing and climbed up to sit on the highest rail. "Now what do we do?"

"I was just thinking about that. How about if we find some string or something to tie around his collar, and we can take him for a walk around the neighborhood and see if any of the neighbors know who he belongs to? I don't remember seeing him in the neighborhood before, but he could be new, or he could be an inside dog."

Jamie nodded. "That sounds like a good idea." He jumped down, placed both hands against his back and arched forward. "Besides, I could use a good walk. All this housework and mystery stuff is giving me a backache."

I knew better than to roll my eyes at him, but I couldn't help myself. He was acting like an eighty-year-old man instead of an eight-year-old boy.

"I'm almost nine," Jamie interrupted.

"What?" I asked, then realized that I had been thinking out loud. "Right," I continued, "let's get this over with. Do you want to watch the dog while I find some string or rope, or would you rather look for something?"

Jamie pointed to the sleeping dog hugging my leg. "He seems to like you more. Plus, he looks pretty comfortable. Why don't you stay here, and I'll try to find something?"

"All right, but don't take too long," I ordered, knowing how easily Jamie got distracted.

Surprisingly, he came back out the door in less than ten minutes. His hands were tucked behind his back, and I feared we were going to have to play one of his silly guessing games. Instead, he surprised me again.

"Will this do?" he asked, drawing a long red leash from behind his back.

"Where did you find that?"

"In the basement. There were some hooks on the wall, and this was hanging on one of them. It's a bit frayed and smells kind of funny, but I thought it would work better than anything else I could find. I pulled most of the spider webs off of it."

"Nice work," I said, holding out my hand to take the leash.

Jamie only smiled.

Unfortunately, our walk was just as unsuccessful as our phone call to the animal shelter had been. No one in the neighborhood seemed to know anything about the dog. No one knew who he belonged to. No one could remember ever seeing him before. So, either this dog appeared out of nowhere, or he was from farther away than we first thought.

Uncertain what else to do, Jamie and I decided to make posters to hang up around town. Scrounging through the desk drawer, I grabbed a handful of markers and a sketch pad and made my way out to the back porch. Since we couldn't take the dog inside, and I didn't want to leave him alone, we decided to work outside. It was a pretty day—a little warm—but at least it wasn't raining.

We spent the next hour or so making posters that read, *Dog Found, brown head with black and white body. If this is your dog, please call 302-555-4719.* They weren't the prettiest posters, but that wasn't important. The only thing that really mattered was finding a home for this dog. Without a camera and the proper computer equipment, we weren't able to attach a photo, but hopefully the description was enough for someone to be able to determine whether or not the lost dog was his.

With the posters in hand, I hooked the leash to the dog's collar, and Jamie and I headed into town. We had made twenty-five posters, so we hung them on every community bulletin board we could find. We pinned the remaining posters on to telephone poles throughout town.

We had hoped to talk to Pop-Pop when we reached the grocery store, but one of the cashiers told us that he was in a very important meeting and could not be disturbed. Not wanting to cause a scene, we left a poster with the cashier and went on our way.

The dog trotted along behind us, obviously interested in all the new sights and smells. If any passersby recognized him, they didn't say anything. I guessed there was nothing left to do but go back to Pop-Pop's and hope that someone called.

As we headed back in that direction, Jamie stopped and turned to me. "Can we get something to eat? I mean, since we're already here in town."

I looked down at my watch and realized that the afternoon was nearly gone. It was, indeed, time to start working on dinner, and it was possible Pop-Pop would be home soon.

"Let's go by the Chinese place and have them fix us some plates to go," I said. "Will that work for you?"

Jamie looked toward the sky and puckered his lips in a strange fashion, twisting them from side to side. "Hmm," he said, rubbing his stomach, "yeah, I think Chinese sounds good, but only if I can get an extra egg roll."

"Fine," I said, pulling out my wallet to make sure I had the money that Pop-Pop had left for us. I had intended to put it in my wallet, but with all the commotion[5], I couldn't remember if I had actually done it.

Relieved to find the money, I led the way to the Chinese place and ordered dinner for the three of us while Jamie waited outside with the dog.

As soon as I exited the restaurant, Jamie jumped up from the bench on which he had been sitting. "What about him?" He pointed down at the dog.

"I told you, Jamie. We'll just have to hope someone calls and claims him."

"No," he said, shaking his head. "I mean, what's he going to eat. Pop-Pop doesn't have any dog food, does he?"

I hadn't thought about that. "Well, I would assume since he doesn't have a dog that he won't have any dog food. I guess we'll need to get some while we're in town. The pet store is on the way home. We'll stop there and get a couple of cans."

"Just a couple of cans?"

"Yes," I replied firmly. "Jamie, you can't get attached to this dog. He's going to have to go back to his owner, or we'll have to find him another home soon. We can't keep him. We've been through this."

Jamie reached down to pet the dog's head. "I know. I just thought we might have him a little longer than that."

Not wanting to disappoint him any more than I already had, I put my hand on his shoulder and said, "We'll see, Jamie. For now, let's just get a couple of cans of dog food and go home so we can see if anyone calls."

When Pop-Pop arrived home that evening, we explained about the dog and our attempts to find his owner. He agreed to let the dog stay inside with us until we could find who he belonged to. After feeding the dog, we piled up some pillows to make a bed on the laundry room floor. Pop-Pop placed a bowl of water next to the bed, then quietly closed the door to the laundry room. I expected the dog to cry, but he didn't make a sound.

"I don't know why he can't sleep in my room," Jamie whined.

Pop-Pop turned to him with a patient expression. "First off, we don't know that he's house-trained, which means he might make a mess up there on the carpets. Second, he's a flighty thing. The last thing we want to do is put him in a strange place at the top of a steep set of stairs. He could fall and hurt himself."

Jamie didn't say anything, but it was obvious he was upset. Strangely, seeing him so disappointed was breaking my heart, so I tried to think of a way to make him feel better. I was struggling to come up with something when, suddenly, I remembered about Maria and my hunch about the thunderstorm.

"Pop-Pop, would it be possible for you to drop us off at Maria's house tomorrow morning before work?"

Jamie's face lifted, and I noticed a familiar twinkle in his eye.

"Well," Pop-Pop said as he settled into his easy chair, "I guess so, but I have to be there early. Do you think Maria and her uncle would mind having guests so early in the morning?"

I hadn't thought of that. "I can call and ask, but if it's okay with her, could you drop us off?"

Pop-Pop knew better than to answer without asking a few questions of his own. "Why do you want to go to Maria's tomorrow? What's this all about?"

I spent the next half hour explaining my theory[6] and why I felt it was important to talk with Maria again. I assured our grandfather that we would be responsible and would obey Maria's uncle–the one who was staying with her until her father was found, *if* her father was found. When I felt I had explained things the best that I could, I stopped talking and waited for Pop-Pop's answer.

He sat in thought for several moments, then spoke. "What about your new little friend? He can't stay here by himself all day."

The puppy. How had I so quickly forgotten about the puppy? I guess the same way I had nearly forgotten about Maria today. It seems my brain is only big enough for one mystery at a time.

"When I call Maria, I could ask if it's okay if we bring the dog with us," I answered.

Pop-Pop nodded. "Call her now before it gets too late, and make sure she checks with her uncle. Max is a very nice gentleman, so I'm sure he'll be fine with it, but it's always polite to ask. If he says it's okay, I'll give you a ride over there tomorrow, but how are you planning to get home?"

"You could come get us," Jamie chimed in.

"If you don't mind," I added, not wanting to put more pressure on Pop-Pop. I knew he had a lot going on, and I had no desire to make things worse for him.

"I don't mind," Pop-Pop said with a smile. "Go call Maria, and let me know what she says."

It didn't take me long to make the call. I wish I could describe to you the relief I felt when her uncle said that we could come and bring the dog too, but I wouldn't even know how to explain it. Let's just say I thought I might be able to sleep that night.

Meanwhile. . .

What have I gotten myself into? the man thought as he shifted his weight, then winced at the immediate pain that shot through his leg. How many times had he told his daughter, Maria, to think before she acted? How many times had he warned her about the danger of not thinking things through? He knew better. He had been trained to survive in all manner of situations, but who would have thought it would ever come to this? It was all a big mistake—a very big mistake. A mistake that may yet cost him his life.

Chapter Four:
It's All in the Name

As eager as I was to talk to Maria, my body protested[7] the early awakening. Since we'd been staying here in Delaware with Pop-Pop, Jamie and I had taken to sleeping in most mornings. Getting up at seven in the morning was quite a shock to my system. Still, once my mind kicked into gear, I couldn't wait to share with Maria my suspicions about the thunderstorm.

After a quick breakfast, the three of us, plus one dog, headed out the door and made our way to Maria's house. When we arrived, the porch light was on, and both Maria and her uncle were waiting at the door to welcome us.

Pop-Pop pulled into the driveway and waved at the couple on the porch. Without turning off the ignition, he turned to us. "You kids be good and do what you're told. I'll be back to pick you up around six this evening."

Jamie and I nodded, then crawled out of the vehicle, carefully lowering the puppy down from the seat of the tall truck. Jamie had brought nothing for the day, but I, as usual, had insisted on bringing my emergency bag. Not knowing what the day might hold, I filled the bag a little fuller than usual. It contained snacks (of course), a couple of sodas, a couple of bottles of water, the dog's leash and some dog biscuits we'd decided to buy at the store. I had also packed a notepad, pen and a book, in case I grew bored as the day wore on. In the hopes that we might be able to explore the trails, I decided to wear my tennis shoes.

After scrounging through the bag for a moment, I hefted it onto my shoulder then bent down to attach the leash to the dog's collar. We had still not received any calls about the poor pup, and I was beginning to wonder if the little guy had any family at all. On top of that, I was growing tired of calling him *the dog* or *the puppy*. The thought crossed my mind that perhaps we should give him a name . . . just until we'd found him a home, that is.

We waved good-bye to Pop-Pop as he pulled out of the drive, and then turned to greet Maria and her uncle, who invited us inside after a few minutes of petting and playing with our new little friend.

"Would you kids like anything to eat?" Maria's uncle asked.

"No, sir," I replied. "We ate before we left." I hesitated, not sure how to ask the next question. "I'm sorry, but I don't think I know your last name. Obviously, if you're Mr. Baker's brother, then your name would also be Mr. Baker, but if you're Maria's mother's brother, then I don't know what your name would be. I'm sorry. I know I should have asked sooner, but with the mysterious disappearance and all, I guess my mind has been a little preoccupied. Pop-Pop just calls you Max, but my mom would have a cow if I called you by your first name."

The man smiled. He had a handsome face and kind eyes that crinkled at the edges. "Beth, that is, Maria's mother, was my sister. My name is Max Solomon." He held out his hand, and I shook it.

"Nice to meet you, Mr. Solomon. I'm sorry to hear about your sister."

The crinkles around his eyes disappeared as his smile transformed into a frown. "Thank you. It's been difficult without her. We were very close."

A sniffle caught my attention, and I turned to see Maria standing just behind me with tears in her eyes.

"It was so hard to lose her," she cried, "and now to lose my father too. I just . . . don't . . . know . . ." Her words broke into sobs.

I wrapped my arms around her. "I'm so sorry, Maria. I know this is difficult, but we will find him. That's why we're here."

Jamie blurted, obviously uncomfortable with all the tears, "Yeah, Abby's got a good idea where we can look for your father."

Maria's sobs slowly eased, and when she could finally catch her breath, she pulled back from my embrace. "Really? You think you know where to find him?"

"Not exactly," I admitted, "but I do have an idea. How about we go sit down somewhere comfortable, and I'll tell you all about it?"

Maria nodded, and Mr. Solomon led the way to a small, but comfortable den. Though the room only contained a coffee table and a couch, the couch was one of those L-shaped ones and had plenty of room for all of us to sit. Unlike many couches I've sat on, this one didn't try to swallow me. It was actually quite comfortable.

In the quiet of the morning, I explained my idea to Maria and Mr. Solomon. I told them about the thunderstorm and how it reminded me of the storm we had right after we arrived in Delaware.

"Do you remember if there was a storm on the day your father went missing?" I asked.

Before I had finished the question, Maria was nodding. "Yes, yes, I remember now. There was a storm late that afternoon. I remember because I was home alone and, though storms don't usually scare me, I was afraid. I kept looking up at the clock to see when Daddy was going to get home, but the time passed . . ." she paused, ". . . and he never came home."

Though I could sense her sadness, a smile of satisfaction spread across my face. Finally, a lead! But before I allowed myself to indulge[8] in the idea, I needed to clear up a few more things.

"Did you tell the police about the storm, or did any of them mention anything to you about the possibility of your father finding shelter from the storm?"

Maria thought for a moment. "No, I didn't say anything about the storm. When Daddy didn't come home that night, I called Uncle Max. He came and got me, and we went to the police station. The police said that we couldn't file a missing person's report until he had been gone for twenty-four hours. By the time we finally filled out the report, I was so upset that I had completely forgotten about the storm. I didn't even mention it." She turned to her uncle. "Did you, Uncle Max?"

He shook his head. "No, sweetie, I don't think I did. I told the police what I knew about Dan's plans for the day and about the call from you when he didn't come home, but I didn't think about the storm either." He shifted his weight on the couch and leaned in so that he could see all three of us. "I do remember, however, that one of the officers said they had checked all the surrounding houses and buildings, even the abandoned ones. They didn't find anything."

Hope fled as quickly as it had risen, but before its deadly tentacles could grip my heart, Jamie spoke up.

"What about mines?" he asked. "If he didn't go to a building or cabin, what about an old mine? People in the movies always find a mine or a cave when they're trapped in a storm. He could have done the same, right?"

Mr. Solomon shook his head again. "I'm sorry, Jamie, but I don't think there are any caves or mines around here. I know there are a few rock quarries, but they're above ground and wouldn't really offer protection from a storm. Other than that, I can't think of any 'non-building' place he might find refuge in."

Noticing the fallen look on Jamie's face, Mr. Solomon continued. "But it was a very good idea. I don't think the police thought of that one." He winked and smiled at Jamie, causing my brother to smile in return.

After a little more discussion, Mr. Solomon agreed to go with us to explore the trails later on in the day. I was eager to get out there, but I also understood that he had other obligations. From what Maria had told us, her uncle made his living as a freelance copywriter. He enjoyed the work and seemed to be very good at it, but from what I understood, when someone worked as a freelancer[9], he took work when it came and honored the deadlines set by the clients. That was the situation Mr. Solomon was currently in. He had work to do and deadlines to meet. Nevertheless, he promised, whether his work was done or not, to drive us out to the trails after lunch.

With a few hours to kill, Jamie and I decided it would be a good idea to walk the dog. After all, we had no idea whether or not he was house-trained, and it would be very embarrassing if he had an accident at Maria's house.

As I rose from the couch, the dog leaped to his feet, almost as if he knew what was coming. Turning to our hostess, I asked, "Maria, is there somewhere we can walk our dog? I'm sure he's getting restless, and he probably needs to use the bathroom."

Maria smiled. "Sure. We can all go for a walk around the neighborhood. Daddy and I do it all the time, and since you're almost a grown up, Abby, I'm sure Uncle Max won't mind if we go without him. By the way, what's your dog's name?"

"He's not ours," Jamie said as he attached the leash to the dog's collar. "We found him behind our grandfather's house, and we're just keeping him until someone claims him."

Maria nodded. "Oh, so what do you call him?"

For some reason, I felt ashamed. "We just call him *the dog* or *the puppy*, but I've been thinking about giving him a real name—just until we find his family."

Maria clapped her hands together. "Ooh, maybe we could think of a name while we walk. It'll be like a game. I love games."

Jamie and I both smiled, happy that the poor girl had something to bring her cheer during this dark time.

As we walked, the topic of choosing a name for the dog seemed to last forever. Maria threw out one name after another. Good names. Strange names. It didn't seem to matter to her. If it crossed her mind, she blurted it out. Can you believe she actually suggested the name *Cat?* What kind of person would name a dog *Cat?* Sadly, that was one of her better suggestions. I was just about to decide that the dog didn't need a name after all when he barked. It was the first time he had done so since we had found him, and it startled me. To be such a young dog, he had a deep, ferocious[10] bark.

"What's he barking at?" Jamie asked.

Uncertain, I watched the dog for a moment. His ears were pulled back as if listening to some sound that only he could hear. His back was stiff and straight, his tail lifted high in the air. His nose sniffed the air in between short barks and menacing[11] growls.

He had paused in front of a small gray house that looked as ill-kept[12] as the yard in which it sat. The house resembled a crinkled box with a small triangular section of roof that stretched out above a small brick porch. The siding peeled away from the house like the skin of an onion, revealing rotted wood underneath. The white trim was chipped and broken. The large, three-paned window was shattered, leaving gaping holes where the glass had fallen out. The burgundy door sat crooked on its hinges.

The yard itself was a tangle of bushes and briers and grass. Wild foliage reached up to the windows and beyond, completely obscuring the backyard, if there was one. The fencing on either side of the house was bent and battered. All in all, the place was a mess. I sincerely hoped that it had been abandoned a long time ago. I couldn't imagine anyone living in a place like that.

I turned away from the house and shrugged. "It's just an old, abandoned house. I don't think there's anything to worry about."

"Then why is the dog still barking?" Jamie asked.

"And what's that smell?" questioned Maria.

My senses kicked into gear. The dog's growls grew more intense, and there was a strange odor in the air. Not necessarily stinky, but very unusual, like something I had never smelled before. "I don't know. I smell it too. Have you never noticed it before, Maria?"

Maria held her forearm across her nose and shook her head. "I've seen the house," she said in a nasally tone, "but I've never smelled that before."

Eager to get away from the stench (and the empty house that was beginning to give me the creeps), I tugged on the leash. "Come on, boy. Let's go."

For a moment, the dog pulled against me, intent on barking at the house. Then he finally came along, stopping every few steps to turn back and growl, as if something were following us.

"That was weird," Jamie said as we made our way farther down the street.

"It sure was," Maria agreed. After a moment of silence, she said, "Let's get back to choosing a name for the dog."

I rolled my eyes and sighed inwardly. "Actually, I had an idea. Jamie and I have two cats who are named after kitchen appliances. One is named

Blender. The other is *Mixer.* Maybe we could name the dog something like that too."

"Great idea! We could call him *Microwave,*" Jamie shouted, "or *Can Opener.*"

I grimaced, thinking that Maria's idea of *Cat* was better than either of those options. "No, I don't think either of those will work," I said in the nicest voice I could manage. "Got any other ideas?"

Suddenly, Maria stopped and grabbed my arm. At first, I was alarmed, thinking something had happened or that I was about to step on a snake or something. I jerked to a halt.

"I've got it!" she screamed, a huge smile on her face. "Have you ever heard of Sherlock Holmes?"

"Who hasn't?" Jamie quipped.

"Well, he was a detective, right? Kind of like the two of you."

I nodded, uncertain of the point she was trying to make.

"Sherlock Holmes had a sidekick named *Watson.* This dog could be your sidekick. Why don't you call him *Watson?*"

Jamie and I exchanged glances and smiled.

"Of course," Jamie said as he leaned down to pet the furry pup. "It makes perfect sense." He rubbed the dog's head and lifted its face upwards. "Hello, Watson. Who's a good boy?"

"Thank you, Maria. You really came through. Watson is the perfect name."

Glad to have that settled, the three us continued our stroll through the neighborhood, counting down the minutes until we could explore the trails and hopefully uncover some shred of evidence that the police had missed.

Chapter Five:
A Hiking We Will Go

After a satisfying lunch of soup and sandwiches, the four of us, plus Watson, climbed into Mr. Solomon's SUV and headed toward the trails. My stomach flip-flopped, both from anticipation and fear. What if we didn't find anything, or worse yet, what if we found Mr. Baker's body? I'd never seen a dead body, and I was pretty sure I didn't want to.

"Which trails do you kids want to explore?" Mr. Solomon asked, interrupting my disturbing thoughts.

"All of them," Jamie answered with enthusiasm.

Mr. Solomon laughed and shook his head. "I don't think you understand. There are more than fifteen miles of trails around the area that my brother-in-law was responsible for. We won't have time to search them all. We have to be off the trails by dusk. Besides, won't your grandfather be stopping by the house to pick you up in a little while?"

Jamie folded his hands in his lap and sat quietly. I could tell by his face he was disappointed, and I knew the feeling. How in the world were we supposed to find a clue when we didn't even know where to look? Mr. Baker could have been anywhere on those fifteen miles of trails the day he disappeared. What were the chances of us choosing the exact same path he took that day?

Turning to Maria's uncle from where I sat in the passenger seat, I said, "We could call Pop-Pop and tell him to not pick us up until later. That would give us until dusk to search more of the trails. It's still not enough time, but it's better than what we would have otherwise."

Mr. Solomon stared through the windshield and said nothing. His mouth twitched, and his forehead creased as if he was thinking hard about something. Finally, he spoke. "How about this? When we get to the park, I'll call your grandfather and see if it's okay for you kids to spend the night with us tonight. Would that be okay?"

I don't know which of us kids looked happier.

"Yes, sir," I replied at the exact moment Jamie shouted, "Awesome!"

Everyone laughed, and we resumed our drive to the park where the tangle of trails began.

After calling Pop-Pop on his cell phone and making arrangements for our sleepover, Mr. Solomon turned off the ignition and signaled for everyone to get out of the vehicle. As I walked around to the driver's side, Mr. Solomon pointed at the bag I hefted over my right shoulder.

"You can leave your bag in the car if you'd like, Abby," he said. "I'll lock the doors. It'll be safe."

"Thanks," I answered, "but this is my emergency bag. I don't go anywhere without it."

Mr. Solomon looked uncertain. "We have a lot of walking to do. Are you sure you want to carry it around with you all day?"

I nodded. "I'm sure."

With a single downward tilt of his head, he seemed to understand that my mind was made up. He slung his own backpack around and threaded his arms through the loops. After securing the clips around his chest and stomach, he motioned for us to follow him. Once again, Maria planted her hand in mine as Jamie struggled to control Watson, who was using his leash to drag Jamie along behind him.

When we arrived at a nearby trail, Mr. Solomon pointed and said, "This is the nearest trail head. How about we start here and just go as far as we can with the time we have?"

The three of us nodded and followed as Mr. Solomon set a moderate[13] hiking pace along the wooded path. As we walked, our surroundings seemed to constantly change. At times it consisted of open grassy meadows or farmland while other times it was more like the trails at home that meandered through the woods and across creeks. Even the walking surfaces changed from time to time, varying from dirt to grass to wood chips. Historic ruins, monuments and even Mason-Dixon[14] markers dotted the area near the trails. Old barns. Rock remnants of some forgotten building. Being the history lover I am, I was excited at each new discovery. So much so, however, that at times I lost sight of our mission.

"What's with all these old buildings and stuff?" Jamie asked as we plodded along.

Mr. Solomon stopped to examine the latest ruin, a crumbling rock structure, its chimney protruding from the middle of the building like a brick hand reaching toward Heaven. "I'm not sure, Jamie. Unfortunately, I don't know a lot about this area."

"You're not from here?" I asked, never taking my eyes from the piece of history before me.

Mr. Solomon shook his head. "No, I'm afraid not. I live down in the southern part of the state, which is where I was born. My house is fairly close to the Delaware/Maryland state line, but I come here a lot to visit. I drove up the night Dan, that's Maria's dad, went missing, and I've been staying with her ever since."

We resumed our walk, and Jamie, still struggling to rein in the rambunctious[15] Watson, broke into a jog in order to catch up with Maria's uncle. "So, have you ever been on these trails?"

"A few times," he answered. "Dan and I have been on several of these trails, but I haven't had the opportunity to walk them all. And I have to admit, I'm not much of a history buff, so all this historical significance stuff doesn't really mean much to me. I'm more interested in the nature side of things. Unique plants, flowing creeks, that sort of thing."

"Me too," Jamie agreed, "but Abby loves history."

Maria, who had fallen behind to get a closer look at some of the ruins, sped up to match my pace. "I like history, too, Abby," she said in a quiet voice.

I smiled and continued to walk, fighting myself with every step to focus on the task at hand. We were looking for clues—anything that suggested Mr. Baker had been on the trail. A button. A pocketknife. A piece of cloth. Anything.

For hours, we plodded along, sometimes at a quick pace, sometimes slower because of tougher terrain. While we never spotted any clues about Mr. Baker's disappearance, I did discover something: Delaware was not as flat as I first thought. There were hills. Not big ones like we have at home. But there were definitely hills. I know because we climbed them, and if you've ever done any hiking, you know that even the smallest hill can take your breath away if you're not used to that kind of exercise.

"What is that?" Maria asked.

Snapping out of my thoughts and struggling to catch my breath from our latest climb, I looked around to see what she was referring to. To my surprise, she wasn't looking or pointing at anything. Instead, she had her eyes closed, her little nose bobbing up and down as she took in short, deep breaths. Before anyone could ask her what she was doing, a familiar smell assaulted my nose.

"I know that smell," I said. "I've smelled it somewhere before." But as hard as I tried, I couldn't remember where.

It was then that I noticed that Watson was behaving oddly. Though he wasn't barking, he was growling deeply. His back was straight and rigid. His tail pointed backward and upward at the same time. The hair on his back stood up, giving it a spiky appearance. His nose wrinkled as he pressed it to the ground then lifted it as if sniffing the air around him. The growl remained steady, never increasing in volume or ferocity. His teeth weren't showing, but it was obvious something had his attention.

I looked at Jamie, who was also sniffing the air and nodding at its familiarity and then at Mr. Solomon who had a look of concern on his face. He sniffed a few times as he pulled his cell phone out of his pocket.

"Great, no signal," he muttered, shoving the phone back into his jeans and reaching into his back pocket. He pulled out a trail map and studied it for several moments, occasionally looking around at our surroundings.

After folding the map and replacing it in his pocket, he placed his index finger over his lips, indicating that we should be quiet. "All right, kids," he whispered, "I'm afraid this trip is over for today."

"But why?" Jamie asked in a tone that was far louder than the one Mr. Solomon had used.

"Ssh," he commanded. "We need to get back to the park office, but we need to do it as quickly and quietly as possible. I promise I'll explain everything when we get there." He placed his finger over his mouth once again, then motioned for us to follow. "Jamie, do what you can to keep Watson quiet. It's important."

After nearly another hour of zig-zagging from one trail to another, we reached the park office. Mr. Solomon insisted we wait in the SUV while he spoke with the man in the office. Whatever he had to say, it didn't take long because within twenty minutes or so, he was striding toward us as we waited in confusion.

"What was that all about?" Jamie asked, obviously unable to contain his curiosity any further.

Mr. Solomon started the engine, put the car into gear and began the drive back to his house. He was quiet for a few minutes, and I began to wonder if he was going to tell us or not. Some adults are funny about not telling kids stuff because they think it'll scare us, but we're really a lot tougher than most people think. Mr. Solomon obviously understood that because he kept his word.

"That smell in the woods was marijuana. It's a drug, and an illegal one at that. Evidently, someone, or maybe more than one person, was hoping to hide out on one of the lesser-used trails and smoke some joints. Unfortunately for that person, we came along. I reported it to the park office, and they called the police. Right now, they're probably searching the area for the criminal."

"But why did we have to be so quiet?" Jamie asked. "Why didn't we just find them ourselves and turn them over to the police? We are detectives after all."

Mr. Solomon shook his head. "No, that would have been dangerous. Something you need to understand about criminals, Jamie, is if they're breaking one law, they're likely to break another. In other words, whoever it was could have had a gun or some other weapon. That's why I wanted everyone to be quiet. I didn't want the druggie to know we were there because I wasn't sure what he'd do if he found out. My goal was to keep everyone safe and report the incident to the proper authorities as soon as possible. I hope you'll make that your goal the next time you're in a situation like this."

"I hope there won't be a next time," I muttered, hugging my emergency bag in my lap. "That was scary! I didn't know why we were in such a hurry or why we had to be so quiet, but I'm glad now that we listened to you. Thank you."

Mr. Solomon looked over and smiled. "You're welcome." He sighed. "Now, let's try to put the whole thing behind us and work on making plans for the evening. You kids still want to stay over?"

"Absolutely," Jamie said as I nodded.

"Okay then. When I called your grandfather, I made arrangements to stop by his house so you two could pick up some clothes and whatever else you need for the evening. Let's go ahead and do that now. Then we'll have the whole evening together. You guys like pizza?"

"Love it!" Jamie cried as he rubbed his stomach, "And I'm starved. All that hiking gave me an appetite."

Everyone laughed as Mr. Solomon said, "Well, I guess we'd better make it *two* large pizzas, huh?

The evening was a lot of fun. We ate pizza, watched movies, played video games and listened to the tales of Mr. Solomon. Being a writer, he had a very good imagination and told some of the best stories I'd heard in a long time.

When he realized, however, that it was almost ten o'clock, he shooed us off to bed. Jamie was set to sleep on the L-shaped couch and had already changed into his pajamas. Watson was allowed to sleep on a large pillow in front of the couch and had, in fact, fallen asleep nearly an hour earlier.

After helping to clean up the mess from the last board game we had played, I followed Maria to her bedroom where I would spend the night.

Just before we shut the door, the phone rang. Mr. Solomon answered, and from the tone of his voice, it wasn't a happy call.

"Do you usually get calls this late at night?" I asked Maria as we both peeked out her bedroom door.

"No," Maria said shortly.

Fearing the worst, the two of us could not help walking back out to the living room once Mr. Solomon had hung up the phone.

"Who was that?" Maria asked.

Mr. Solomon ran his hand through his hair. "It was just the police, sweetie."

Maria's eyes filled with tears. "My daddy?"

Her uncle's face softened as he opened his arms, inviting her into a warm hug. "No, baby, I'm sorry. It wasn't about your daddy. It was about the drug guys today. It turns out there were two of them. The police spotted them, but unfortunately, they got away."

"Did the police get a good look at them? I mean, so they could make wanted posters and stuff like that."

"I'm not sure, Abby. The officer didn't say. He just wanted to thank me for the tip and let me know that the culprits were still on the loose."

"Are we in danger?" Jamie asked from his nest of blankets on the couch.

"Nah," Mr. Solomon said, shaking his head. I don't think the criminals saw us, or they wouldn't have still been there when the police showed up. Everything's fine. The police will find them soon enough." He rubbed Maria's head in a circular motion. "For right now, I know three children who have had a very long day and need to get some sleep."

"Yes, sir," we all said.

Unfortunately, it was easier said than done. All that hiking had certainly tired me out, and my body hurt from all the exercise we'd had. My mind, however, was spinning once again, though this time not about Mr. Baker. Instead, I was reliving the events of the day, particularly the part where we had encountered the druggies, as Mr. Solomon had called them.

Marijuana. I had heard of it. I knew it was bad, and from the smell of it, I couldn't imagine why anyone would want to smoke it. It was a strange odor, like skunks and pine trees and sweet oranges all rolled into one. And the most frustrating part is that it was familiar, but where would I have smelled it before? Was it really the smell I recognized, or was it just similar to something else? Those questions and more kept me awake most of the night.

Chapter Six:
Hmm, That's Not Right

I felt like a zombie at breakfast. Mr. Solomon had been kind enough to get up early and fix a nice meal of bacon, eggs, toast and fruit. It was delicious, but I was so tired from not sleeping much the night before that I barely had enough energy to chew my food.

"So, what do you kids want to do today?" Mr. Solomon asked. "I'm afraid I've got a ton of work to do, but you two are welcome to spend the day here and keep Maria company."

"Oh, yes," Maria exclaimed, "please stay. It's been so nice having other kids to play with."

How could we say "no" to that?

"We'll need to call Pop-Pop and let him know we're staying another day," I said.

"And night?" Maria pleaded.

I looked at Mr. Solomon who smiled and nodded. "We'd be happy to have you stay with us another night."

"Cool!" Jamie said. "I never get to sleep on the couch at home."

After breakfast, I called Pop-Pop and asked about staying another day and night with Maria and her uncle. I could tell from Pop-Pop's voice that he was tired. Evidently, they were working him pretty hard— harder than he had anticipated. Still, he sounded pleased when I told him our plans and agreed to let us stay one more night.

No sooner had Mr. Solomon headed off to his temporary office than Watson trotted over to the back door and let out a loud bark.

Jamie looked at the dog, then back at me. "I think he needs to go to the bathroom."

"So, take him out," I snapped, immediately regretful[16] of my tone. "I'm sorry. I didn't mean to sound rude. I'm just really tired. I didn't sleep well last night."

Jamie didn't respond, but I could tell from his expression that he wasn't upset.

"Why don't we all go for another walk?" Maria suggested. "That way Watson can take care of his potty needs, and we can get a little bit of fresh air and exercise." Turning to stare directly in my eyes, she continued, "It'll make you feel better, Abby. It doesn't make sense, I know, but Momma always said she felt better and had a lot more energy after a nice walk."

To be honest, what I really wanted to do was crawl back in bed, but after looking at the two pairs of eyes (three, if you count Watson's) waiting expectantly for my answer, I realized that wasn't going to happen.

"Jamie, grab the leash. I'll go get my bag."

We decided to do the same circular tour of the neighborhood we had done the day before, only this time we chose to do it in reverse. As much as we had tried to put the events of the previous day behind us, our conversation served as proof that we had been unsuccessful.

"Where do you think the druggies went?" Jamie asked, holding tightly to Watson's leash and attempting to walk at a normal pace, which was difficult since the dog seemed to pull with all his might, eager to run and explore.

"I don't know," I answered, "but they ruined everything."

"What do you mean?" Maria asked, once again placing her hand in mine.

"If it hadn't been for them we would have been able to check out more of the trails. It's bad enough they were breaking the law, but they messed up our plans too. We didn't even get to look at half the trails in the area. Who knows? The clues we're looking for could have been down one of those trails."

Maria nodded but didn't say anything. Jamie continued to fight Watson as the dog pulled and strained against Jamie's weight (which is not much, by the way).

We walked in silence for a while, then an idea struck me. "Maria, your dad has maps of all the trails in the area, doesn't he?"

"Yes," she nodded. "Why?"

"I was just thinking that maybe after our walk we could go look at those maps. We could mark which trails we have already explored and get a good idea of how many trails are left to check. Then maybe we could talk your uncle into taking us up there again to look at the other trails."

"That's a good idea, Abby," Maria said, but her tone didn't sound excited. In fact, she sounded like she was about to cry again. "But Uncle Max can't take us today because he's working."

"Oh," I said as discouragement threatened to overwhelm me.

"Well, maybe we could still look at the maps," Jamie concluded. "I'm sure we can find a way to get back over there soon."

Watson decided to join in the conversation, or at least that's the way it seemed until we realized that his barks were not directed at us.

Once again, we were standing in front of the broken down gray house. And just as before, Watson barked ferociously, the hair on his back standing tall, his eyes alert, and his tail stiff.

"There's that smell again," Maria said, wrinkling up her nose.

The smell! I recognized it immediately and didn't understand why I couldn't place it before. Not only was it the same smell we had noticed the first time we passed this house, but it's also the smell we noticed on the trail—the smell that we later discovered was marijuana.

"That's odd," Jamie said, interrupting my thoughts.

"What?" I whispered, feeling suddenly cautious.

"The door is open," Jamie said. "Does somebody live there?"

Maria shook her head. "I don't think so. I've never seen anybody or any cars or anything. And with the broken windows and everything, I don't see how someone could live there. No, I'm pretty sure it's been abandoned for years."

"Then how did the door get opened?" Jamie questioned. "It wasn't open when we passed by here yesterday."

"No, it wasn't," I agreed.

We walked down the road a little farther so that we could catch a glimpse of the inside of the house. When we reached the proper angle, I nearly lost my breath.

The inside of the house was beautiful —at least, the parts of it that we could see. The walls were covered with a dark red paint and trimmed with white molding. A huge, dark brown fireplace, complete with wrap-around mantle, sat in the center of the wall opposite the door. The floors appeared to be real hardwoods, but the strips of wood were very thin instead of the wide planks I've seen elsewhere. Although a bit dirty, the floors seemed to still be in good condition. In short, the inside of the house seemed to be the exact opposite of the outside. Evidently, Maria thought the same thing.

"How can a house be so ugly and trashy on the outside, yet so nice on the inside?"

A quick look around told me that we were drawing unwanted attention from the neighbors. Eyes peeked through openings in doorways and slits in the window blinds, no doubt trying to figure out why our dog was barking like a maniac and why the three of us were standing in the middle of the road like a bunch of idiots.

"I think we need to keep moving," I whispered in between Watson's growls.

"But I want to get a closer look," Jamie protested.

I grabbed his arm and pulled him closer so I could be certain he could hear me above the noise. "Not now, Jamie. We'll come back later, but for now, it might not be safe. Let's go."

Jamie nodded, then pulled on Watson's leash. The dog balked. "Watson, let's go!"

As he had done before, Watson followed, stopping every few steps to turn and growl at the strange house that reeked of marijuana.

"Did you recognize the smell?" I asked when we had turned the corner onto Maria's street.

"It smelled like a skunk!" Maria exclaimed.

"I thought it smelled like one of those herbal shops Mom likes to go in," Jamie confided, "but there was something else too. Kind of skunk-like, but not really."

"I'm not certain, but I'm pretty sure it was marijuana."

"You're right," Jamie said. "That did smell just like the stuff in the woods yesterday."

Maria nodded. "Yes, it did. I thought it was familiar, but I also thought it smelled like a skunk, and unfortunately, I've smelled plenty of those. But you're right, Jamie. There's something else besides the skunk scent." Turning to me, she asked, "What should we do? Should we call the police?"

I hesitated. "Maybe, but what if we're wrong? We'll look like idiots."

"But, Abby," Jamie protested, "we have to do something. There could be some kind of drug operation going on in that house."

"You watch too much television," I said.

"Maybe," he answered, "but think about it. The smell of marijuana. A house that's supposed to be abandoned. The door standing open when it wasn't that way yesterday. I'm telling you, it sounds fishy to me. I think we ought to tell somebody."

"We will," I said, "but let's take a look first just to make sure we're right."

"Fine," Jamie conceded, "let's go."

As we approached the steps to Maria's house, I paused. "Not now. We'll go tonight after it gets dark. That way we can have the element of surprise. If there is someone in there, they won't see us coming."

"But if we wait until dark, how will we see where we're going?" Maria asked.

Placing my hands on my hips, I stood as tall and grownup as I could. "You're not coming with us."

"What? But why?"

"Because," I explained, "it's too dangerous. We have no idea what's going on in that house. Jamie could be right. There could be drug dealers in there or worse. It's best if you stay here. Besides, we'll need you to cover for us if your uncle suspects anything."

"But I could help," Maria argued.

"I know, but the help we need is for you to stay here and take care of things with your uncle. If he finds out what we're up to, he'll be angry. We need you to make sure he doesn't find out. Can you do that?"

Maria sighed and nodded. "Yes," she whispered, "I can do that."

I turned my gaze toward Jamie. "She does have a good point, though. If we use flashlights to see, we'll give ourselves away. How are we going to stake out the house if we can't see anything?"

Jamie smiled a curious smile. I couldn't decide if it was amusing or scary. "Leave that to me!"

Meanwhile. . .

The man was uncertain what would drive him mad first: the pain or the incessant dripping somewhere in the distance. True, the source of the drip was probably the only thing saving him from total dehydration, but for days it had been the one sound that seemed to drown out all the rest. He missed the familiar sounds of laughter and music. He missed Maria's attempts to sing along as he hummed his favorite hymn. The last thought created a pool in his eyes from which tears began to pour. He brushed the tears from his cheeks with the back of his right hand, cleared his throat the best he could and began to sing in a hoarse, raspy voice. "Through many dangers, toils and snares I have already come; 'Tis grace that brought me safe thus far, and grace will lead me home." With a small smile, he drifted off to sleep.

Chapter Seven:
The Pirate Spies

As the evening slowly passed, I began to wonder if Mr. Solomon was ever going to go to bed. He had been busy in his office since dinner that night, but I knew we couldn't chance sneaking out until he had gone to sleep, especially with Jamie sleeping on the couch and Watson sleeping on the floor beside him. No, it was best that we wait, but as the minutes ticked by, I found myself growing more sleepy. I feared that if we didn't go soon, I was going to fall asleep, and our chance of checking out the house would be lost.

Finally, around midnight, Mr. Solomon made his way to the bedroom and shut the door behind him. I waited another twenty minutes or so to make sure he wasn't going to come back out for anything, then rose and put on my shoes. I hadn't changed into my pajamas, so after lacing up my tennis shoes, I grabbed my bag and made my way toward the door.

"Be careful," came a sleepy voice from the other bed.

"Maria, I didn't know you were still awake."

Maria shifted in the bed and rubbed her eyes. "I've been dozing on and off, but when you got up, the bed squeaked and woke me up again."

"Sorry. We'll be back soon," I whispered. "If you hear or see your uncle, you know what to do, right?"

Maria nodded.

As quietly as I could, I slipped out into the hallway and pulled the door closed behind me. Creeping down the hallway, I secured my bag over my right shoulder. The bag was lighter than usual, which I felt was necessary for this type of operation. It still contained a couple of snacks and juice boxes, but other than two flashlights, a pack of tissues and a small pair of binoculars I had borrowed from Maria, the bag was fairly empty.

When I reached the living room, I noticed Watson was snoring away, his head hanging off the edge of the pillow on which he slept and his little feet twitching. Some watch dog he'd be! Despite the sleeping mutt, Jamie was already up and lacing his shoes. He wore an eye patch over one eye, giving him the appearance of the world's smallest pirate. As he stood, he held out a similar eye patch.

"Here you go," he said.

"Why would I want to wear that?" I asked in hushed tones, "and where did those come from anyway?"

"You're not the only one who has an emergency bag," Jamie replied. "I just happen to keep a few items of my own. Secret spy watch. Eye patches. Pocketknife. Just the usual. After all, you never know what we detectives will run into."

Unfortunately, I was all too familiar with my brother's collection of spy gear, but at the moment, I was struggling to figure out how the eye patches fit into the picture.

"Okay," I said, "the spy gear I get, but what's with the patches. How do they help us?"

A cough sounded from the back bedroom, followed by the sounds of squeaky bed springs. Jamie and I looked at each other in alarm and stood as still as statues. Within a moment, the sounds stopped, and Jamie and I each let out a heavy breath.

I nodded my head toward the door. "Let's take this outside. You can tell me all about the eye patches then."

We crept to the door, gingerly unbolted the lock, then slipped onto the porch, closing the door gently behind us. For safe measure, we made our way down the steps and stood at the edge of the yard.

Jamie placed the extra eye patch in my hand. "This is really cool. You're gonna love this."

I stared at the eye patch, thinking that nothing he could say could interest me enough to make me want to wear the ridiculous costume.

"I saw a show once where they tested this idea about pirate eye patches," he went on.

"How did I know this was something you saw on television?" I interrupted.

"Just let me finish," Jamie said with some impatience. "What they found out is that if you cover your eye with a patch like this," he pointed at his patch-covered eye, "your eye will get adjusted to the dark. Aggravated, I think they called it."

"Acclimated[17]," I corrected, rolling my eyes.

"Right, acclimated. Anyway, the covered eye gets used to the dark, so when you get in a dark room or something like that, all you have to do is take off the patch, and you'll be able to see in the dark. Actually, it works best if you cover the other eye with the patch because it hasn't adjusted to the dark yet. That's how pirates were able to go from the bright light above deck on their ships to the dark areas below deck. They just switched the patch from one eye to the other and let the adjusted eye see in the dark. That's probably why so many pirates had patches. Not because they were missing an eye or had an injury, but so that they could see in the dark. Pretty cool, huh?"

Admittedly, it was very cool. I only hoped it worked as well as Jamie claimed. Otherwise, our exploration of the suspected drug house was going to be short and uneventful. I reluctantly placed the eye patch over my right eye and led the way down the street. Fortunately, the street lights provided ample light for walking down the road, so we were able to leave the flashlights in my bag.

As we drew closer to the house, my stomach began to twist and turn. For some reason, the true danger of this little quest didn't hit me until we were nearly at our destination. But when it hit, it hit hard. What were we doing? What if we found something? Or worse yet, what if something found us? For the first time all day, I was beginning to think this was a very bad idea.

"Do you smell it?" Jamie whispered as the house came into view.

I nodded, but then remembering that he probably couldn't see me in the dark, I muttered, "Yeah. It's not as strong as it was before, but it's definitely still there."

The house was dark, both within and without. Not only were there no lights shining through the windows, but the nearest streetlight was far enough away and at such an angle that its light couldn't work its way through the tangle of trees and bushes surrounding the house. Flashlights were definitely out of the question since they might attract attention, and as we moved closer to the house and under the shadow of the trees, I feared we wouldn't be able to see well enough to investigate at all.

"Okay," Jamie whispered. "Let's switch our patches to the other eye. We should be able to see better then."

As we sneaked around to the back of the house, the darkness grew and threatened to drive away my remaining courage. I stopped under the cover of a bush and moved my eye patch over to my left eye. After blinking a moment to get rid of the blurriness in my right eye, I realized that Jamie's plan had worked. It was like someone had flipped on a light. Not a bright light, but more like a nightlight. What was nearly impossible to see just a moment ago was now crystal clear. I guess you can learn a few things from television, but I prefer to stick to my books.

With our new-found sight, we easily maneuvered[18] to the nearest window at the back of the house and peered in. This window, unlike those at the front, was actually intact. From what we could see, the room contained a couple of large tables, each piled high with a variety of bags and plastic containers. Most of the bags were empty, but a couple of them on the end of the second table were packed full of something. I squinted to make out the items.

"What's in those bags at the end of the table there?" I asked Jamie, pointing at the filled bags. "Can you tell?"

Jamie squinted with his one eye in the direction I had pointed. "That one looks like a bunch of markers or maybe highlighters, but the other one, I can't really tell. It kind of looks like candy."

I nodded. "Yeah, that's what I thought too." I scanned the room once more and noticed a small pile hiding behind a stack of plastic dishes. It appeared to be a stack of small bags filled with something that looked a lot like grass. I had only seen drugs on television, but I was pretty sure I knew what those little bags contained and what they were intended for. "Let's move down to the next window."

The next window was a narrow window that was too high off the ground for Jamie to be able to look through. I even had to stand on my tiptoes to peer in.

It was a bathroom, and a small bathroom at that. A simple sink and toilet sat against the left wall, and directly across from that was a skinny bathtub. I couldn't see the entire tub because it seemed to stretch all the way to the same wall that the window was on, and since I couldn't really see straight down, the end of the tub was blocked from my view.

What I could see, however, was a strange contraption[19] stretched across the tub. I really couldn't figure out what it was or what it was supposed to do, but it had a lot of wires and tubing running out of it. Whatever it was, it didn't belong in the bathroom. Something was definitely not right in this place.

"What do you see?" Jamie whispered up at me.

"I'm not sure," I confessed, "but I think there's something very strange going on here. Let's see what else we can find, then we need to get back before Mr. Solomon finds out we're missing."

There was one last window on the back side of the house, and unlike the previous window, this one was placed nearly at ground level, like maybe it was the window of a basement. In order to look in, we both had to get down on the ground. Jamie stretched out on his stomach while I sat on my knees and leaned down to peek through the glass. Unfortunately, this glass seemed to be coated on the inside with some sort of glaze or frosting, making it impossible for us to see anything.

"Do you hear that?" Jamie asked.

I stilled my racing heart and listened for anything out of the ordinary. "The dripping?" I asked.

"Yeah," he replied. "Where do you think it's coming from?"

I pressed my ear closer to the low window. The volume of the dripping increased. "It's coming from in there," I pointed to the window and the room that lay beyond it.

Jamie shifted his position and propped himself up on his elbows, resting his chin in his hands. "What do you think it is? Could it be another clue as to what's going on in there?"

"I don't know," I admitted. "It's probably just a faucet dripping or something like that." I sat quiet for a moment. "I wish we could see in there, but I think it's safe to say that whatever is going on here is not legal. We need to tell Mr. Solomon."

"But he'll know we sneaked out," Jamie protested in a volume that sounded like a scream in the silence of the night.

"Shh," I whispered. "You're going to get us in trouble before we even have a chance to talk to Mr. Solomon."

Jamie looked uncertain.

"We have to tell him, Jamie. Then he can decide whether or not to call the police."

Jamie nodded. "All right. I just hope he isn't mad, and I really hope he doesn't tell Pop-Pop."

With a grimace, I said, "Well, I wouldn't hold your breath on that one. Come on, let's get out of here. This place is giving me the creeps."

As we reached the road, the streetlights seemed brighter than they had earlier. Remembering the eye patch I still wore, I pulled it off my face and blinked again to clear away the blurry sensation. Handing the patch to Jamie, I said, "Good idea with these patches. They really helped a lot. Thanks."

Jamie beamed. There had been a time when that smug look of his would have made me angry, but now it only made me smile. Sure, he may be a pest at times, but as little brothers go, he isn't really that bad. . . but don't tell him I said so.

After we arrived at the Baker's house and tiptoed back to our sleeping areas, I changed into my pajamas and crawled into bed. Maria slept soundly in the bed opposite mine, so I assumed that meant that we had not been discovered. But that would change soon enough.

Despite my fatigue, I couldn't get to sleep. As I tossed and turned, I couldn't shake the image of the things we had seen in the house that night. I didn't know much about drug operations, but I could imagine that each of the things we saw could be related to drugs. And as for those little bags full of the grassy substance, well, even I had seen enough television to know that those looked like drugs.

But as much as those thoughts plagued my mind, there was another thought that made those seem like pleasant dreams. It was a thought that had struck me as we hurried home from our stakeout. What if we weren't the first ones to stumble across this drug operation? What if Mr. Baker had found out? After all, he did work on the trails where the drug users were almost caught the other day, and now we were pretty sure that someone was making drugs right there in Mr. Baker's neighborhood. What if he noticed the smell and thought to do some investigating of his own? And what if he got caught? What would druggies do to someone like that—someone who could turn them over to the police? Was it possible that they had him tied up somewhere, maybe in that basement? Or worse, would they have gotten rid of him for good?

My stomach churned as much as my thoughts did. On the one hand, I was excited that we might have finally solved the case of Maria's missing father. On the other hand, I wasn't sure that I was ready to face the fact that he might be dead. Still, I knew what I had to do. First thing in the morning, I had to tell Mr. Solomon everything about the house and my suspicions about Mr. Baker. He'd have to take it from there.

In the meantime, I decided to pray. I prayed for Mr. Baker, wherever he was, that God would keep him safe and give him comfort. I prayed for Maria who hadn't yet gotten over losing her mom and was now facing the possibility of losing her dad too. I prayed for Mr. Solomon, who had left his own family to do what he could for his brother-in-law. And lastly, I prayed for Pop-Pop, that God would give him the strength to do the work that he now faced.

Usually, praying puts me to sleep, especially when I'm tired, but not this night. Instead, I stared at the ceiling and tried to keep my thoughts from running away with me again. Through the process, one thought kept jumping out: *It looks like I won't be getting much sleep again tonight.*

Chapter Eight:
Busted!

Once again, morning came far too early. Even so, I was both eager and anxious to talk to Mr. Solomon. I knew Jamie and I were going to be in trouble for sneaking out the night before, and I was prepared to face the consequences. My only prayer was that our efforts had not been in vain and that our exploration might lead to the capture of some criminals . . . and possibly the discovery of Maria's father.

After dressing, I hurried downstairs, leaving Maria sleeping peacefully in her bed. I hoped Jamie had kept our deal about telling Mr. Solomon together, but as I reached the living room, I realized I had nothing to fear. Though Mr. Solomon was busy fixing breakfast in the adjoining kitchen, Jamie slept soundly. Figured! That boy could sleep through a tornado.

Watson was actually awake this time, though he made no attempt to move from his pillow. He merely watched me as I entered the room, shifting his eyes to follow my movements but never lifting his head.

"Good morning," Mr. Solomon said. "Did you sleep well?"

Why do people always ask me that? I didn't want to lie, but I wasn't ready to tell Mr. Solomon the truth either. After all, I had made a promise to Jamie, who was thankfully beginning to stir on the couch.

"Um, well, not really," I admitted. "In fact, if you'll give me just a minute to get Jamie up, there's something we need to talk to you about."

Mr. Solomon looked both amused and concerned. "Okay, I'll be right here when you're ready."

I strode over to the couch and pulled Jamie's cover from him. Shaking him gently by the shoulder, I tried to convince him to get up. "Come on, Jamie. We need to talk to Mr. Solomon."

"Now?" he whined as he groped around with one hand for his blanket.

"Yes, now." I lowered my voice to a whisper and leaned closer to him. "The longer we wait, the more likely that the criminals will be able to sell their drugs or escape. We need to tell Mr. Solomon."

Jamie groaned, stretched, then rose to a seated position. "Can I at least change out of my pajamas first?"

"Yes, but don't be long. I want to get this over with."

Seated at the table with Mr. Solomon, Jamie and I spilled out our entire tale.

"You did what?" Mr. Solomon asked. "Do you have any idea what kind of danger you put yourselves in? You kids could have been kidnapped, injured or even killed. You two are old enough to know better. What in the world got into you?"

The more he spoke, the angrier he became. His voice rose from a conversational tone to a near shout. But I understood. After all, he was right. What we did was dangerous and stupid. We should have just called the police when we suspected something was up.

"We're sorry," Jamie mumbled.

"It was my fault," I jumped in. "It was my idea to check out the house. Jamie wanted to call the police, but I was afraid that if we were wrong, the police would be upset or worse that people would make fun of us. We're supposed to be detectives after all, and I guess I was so worried about protecting our pride that I didn't really consider all the risks. It was a foolish thing to do, and I am really sorry." I paused for a moment, unsure how to continue. "But Mr. Solomon, even though it was wrong, we can't ignore what we saw. There's definitely a drug operation going on in that house, and . . ." Again, I couldn't seem to find the words I was looking for. Whether I was embarrassed or scared, I couldn't tell, but my mouth felt dry and my throat raw. After swallowing a few times, I finally continued, "And I was wondering if it might be possible that Mr. Baker stumbled upon this operation. I mean, it's right here in his neighborhood, and we know there were some other drug users on the trails just a few days ago. What if he was on to them?"

Mr. Solomon held up his hand. "That's a lot of assumption, Abby. I don't deny that it's possible, but do you have any proof? What makes you think such a thing took place?"

Shrinking back in my seat, I lowered my head and shrugged my shoulders. "I don't know. It's just that we couldn't really see what was in the basement of that house. The windows had some sort of coating or something on them. But last night, after we came back, I just had this bad feeling that Mr. Baker might be down there."

"And you say I watch too much television," Jamie muttered.

I glared at him but didn't have the energy for much else. At that moment, Maria came into the room. She glanced around at the three of us, then sighed.

"I guess you told him," she said.

"You knew about this?" Mr. Solomon asked, his tone rising again.

I cringed. Evidently, in the unfolding of our story, I forgot to mention Maria's part in our plan.

"She didn't come with us," I insisted. "I wouldn't let her. But, yes, she knew what we were planning."

Mr. Solomon sat in silence as Maria padded over to the table and sat in the chair beside me. He ran his fingers through his hair and shook his head in such a vigorous manner that I was afraid it would fling across the room. After several moments, he rose and strode over to the telephone.

"This ought to be fun to explain," he fussed as he dialed the police.

Nearly half an hour later, a knock sounded at the door. Mr. Solomon opened it and then ushered in a police officer. The three of us kids sat on the couch— Watson once again on his pillow—and watched as the policeman removed his hat and entered the living room.

"Hello, children," he said, in a much gentler voice than what I was expecting. "I'm Detective Lawrence. I understand you have quite a story to tell."

When we only nodded, Detective Lawrence turned to Mr. Solomon and declared with a smile, "A quiet bunch you've got here."

Mr. Solomon, who I could tell was still angry by the way the muscles twitched in his jaw, smiled a little and answered, "Don't let them fool you, sir. They actually have quite a lot to say."

For the next hour or so, Detective Lawrence asked us questions about our nighttime stakeout. He wanted to know what we saw and who we saw. He asked about the time we had sneaked out and about the first time we had noticed the smell coming from the house. He also had several questions for Mr. Solomon and Maria, but neither of them seemed to know anything beyond what we had told them.

The officer perched on the edge of the sturdy coffee table so that he could talk to all of us face to face. As we talked, he made notes on a little pad he had pulled from one of the many pockets on his belt.

"Is there anything else you kids can think of? Anything else you want to add?"

Jamie shook his head, but I looked up at Mr. Solomon who was already staring directly at me. It was obvious from his expression that he was not going to say anything about my suspicions about Maria's dad. Evidently, he was leaving that decision up to me, but I was torn. I wanted to tell the detective what I thought, but Mr. Solomon was right—I didn't have any proof. Just a silly gut feeling. But was that enough? Besides, with Maria sitting right beside me, did I want to get her hopes up again about finding her father?

Deciding that silence was my best course of action, I shook my head and addressed the police officer. "No, sir. There's nothing else."

As Detective Lawrence folded his notepad closed and placed it in the proper pocket, a voice sounded on his radio. "The scene is secure and the culprits are in custody."

"Roger that," Detective Lawrence spoke in the radio. "I'll be there in five."

Replacing the radio, he looked at us as he rose from the table. "Well, it looks like you kids are heroes. It sounds like the bust was a success." He set his hat back on his head and turned to Mr. Solomon. "Thanks for the call and the information. We'll take it from here. As for you kids," he said turning back to us, "I appreciate your help but don't ever try to take the law into your hands again. No matter how silly it might seem, if you suspect a crime, call the police right away. Don't try to deal with things yourselves. It's dangerous. Do you understand?"

"Yes, sir," we replied.

"Are you going to the drug house now?" Jamie asked, excitement covering any trace of remorse.

"Yes, son. I need to take a look around. That's my job." He winked at Jamie.

"Can we come along?" Jamie pleaded.

The officer shook his head. "I'm sorry. This is a crime scene and no place for children."

Detective Lawrence made his way to the door.

"But what if we could help?" I cried.

He turned back and patted the pocket that contained the notepad he had written on earlier. "I have all the information you've given me. I'm sure it will be very helpful."

"But there's more," I said, deciding that my suspicions about Maria's dad might be the only thing that could gain us access to the crime scene.

"What do you mean more?" the officer asked, taking two strides toward the couch. "I thought you said there wasn't anything else."

I hung my head. "Well, that wasn't entirely true. There is one more thing, but I don't really have any proof, and I didn't want to say anything because I didn't want to upset Maria."

Maria turned to face me. "Me?"

I swallowed hard and told Detective Lawrence my suspicions about Maria's dad, my only proof being the fact that the drug users had been discovered both in the Baker's neighborhood and in the area where Mr. Baker works and the coincidence of the drug operation being discovered shortly after Mr. Baker's disappearance. Maria said she and her dad walked in the neighborhood all the time, but she had never noticed the odd smell coming from the house until the day we were out together.

Despite my uneasiness and the churning of my stomach, I spilled out everything I knew and suspected. Surprisingly, the officer seemed to be taking me seriously. He didn't roll his eyes or accuse me of having a wild imagination, but rather, he pulled out his notepad and began scribbling.

"Well, that does change things a bit," Detective Lawrence said, stuffing his notepad in the pocket once again. He turned to Maria's uncle. "Mr. Solomon, I'll need you to accompany me to the scene of the crime. That way you can identify[20] anything that might belong to your brother-in-law."

Mr. Solomon nodded. "I'll be happy to join you, but I think Maria should come along as well. She would recognize her father's stuff much better than I would."

Maria was still sitting on the couch, obviously thinking about all the events and information that had taken place in the past hour. Her eyes were red, but dry. She looked up at the mention of her name. "Yes, I would like to go. I know my daddy's stuff. I could tell you if he's been there."

Detective Lawrence looked uncertain, but after a moment, he nodded. "Okay, you can all come, but you'll have to stay in the car until I say otherwise, and once you enter the crime scene, it is imperative[21] that you don't touch anything. Do you understand?"

"Yes, sir!" I said, while Jamie and Maria nodded.

"I'm serious, kids. Don't touch anything! It's very important, and you'll need to leave the dog here. We can't have him disturbing the crime scene."

"We understand," I assured him.

After putting on our shoes and closing Watson in the laundry room, the four of us, along with Detective Lawrence, climbed into the police cruiser. I must admit, there's something very uneasy about sitting in the backseat of a police car, and I found myself praying that no one was looking and getting the wrong idea.

When we arrived at the drug house, I was amazed to see the amount of activity taking place. Yellow barricade tape, marked repeatedly with the word *Caution*, surrounded the yard. Four police vehicles with blue lights blazing were parked in front of the house. Officers moved about in the yard, around the cars and in and out of the house. A man with a large camera moved from one area to another, snapping pictures as he went.

Mr. Solomon and the three of us kids sat in the police car as Detective Lawrence entered the house. I'm not sure how long he was gone, but it seemed like an eternity. Finally, he emerged and, spoke to a couple of other police officers for a few minutes, then made his way to the car. He motioned for us to get out, but when I pulled on the door handle, I realized that there was no way for us to get out of the car on our own. The doors were locked, and the door handle didn't even seem to be a real door handle. It was more like a decoration. I looked up helplessly, and Detective Lawrence smiled as he opened the door from the outside.

"As you can see, kids," he said, "you don't ever want to be on the wrong side of the law. When you are, being trapped in a police car becomes the least of your worries."

"I'll remember that," Jamie said, crawling out of the car as quickly as he could.

As we made our way toward the entrance of the house, the officer turned to face us again. "Remember what I told you. Don't touch anything." Turning to look at Maria, he added, "If you see anything that belongs to your father, let me know. Don't pick it up. Just let me know. Okay?"

Maria nodded, and our group entered the house. The smell was five times stronger than what we had smelled earlier. The inside of the house was smoky. Just as we had noticed the day before, the living room was empty except for a few spider webs here and there. The other rooms looked just like we had seen them the night before, with the addition of the many police officers.

Maria studied each room as we went through the house but never identified anything that belonged to her father. By the time we had reached the last room, a corner bedroom, she had tears in her eyes. "It looks like you were wrong, Abby. I don't think he was here. I don't see anything of his."

Detective Lawrence shifted his weight from one foot to the other, then cleared his throat. "There's one room left. Let's go check the basement."

As the officer turned to exit the room, Mr. Solomon reached out and grabbed his arm. "Do you think it's a good idea for them to go? What if. . ." he hesitated and looked back over his shoulder at Maria who was looking down at the floor and wiping a stray tear from her cheek. He lowered his voice, and I strained to overhear him. "What if his body is down there?"

Detective Lawrence peered over Mr. Solomon's shoulder at Maria. "It's okay. My officers have already been down there. There are no surprises like that."

The officer led the way down the hall to a white door that opened in, exposing a narrow set of stairs. There was no railing to hold, but the wall offered plenty of support for going down the steps. When we reached the bottom, I couldn't believe my eyes.

There were potted plants of many different sizes. Fluorescent lamps hung at various angles from the ceiling. Large black bags that looked like portable closets stood in three of the four corners. A large plastic sink, filled halfway with water, occupied the final corner of the large room. Water from the faucet above dripped steadily into the pool of liquid, reminding me of the incessant dripping sound we had noticed the night before.

"This was a full-scale operation," Detective Lawrence said. "These guys were running a complete business. From the looks of things, they grew, processed and sold the marijuana from these very premises22. We found bags of the substance in one of the other rooms, along with some magic markers and candy. We believe the markers and candy were part of their distribution plan."

"Markers and candy? How does that help with distribution?" I asked.

"Well, Abby," the detective said, "a lot of time these criminals will place drugs in a small bag, then empty out a marker and put the drugs inside the hollowed out marker. This way they can pass the drugs around without arousing suspicions. As for the candy, I'm afraid they may have been lacing it with the drug. If so, I can only assume they were planning to distribute it, possibly to children like yourselves. Candy laced with marijuana doesn't have the same smell as marijuana that is smoked in a pipe or as a joint. Drug dealers get kids hooked on drugs by offering them candy like this, and the really bad part is that the poor kids don't even realize what's happening until it's too late. Unfortunately, criminals tend to be smart and find all sorts of ways to make money and sell their goods."

"I had no idea," Jamie said. "I never thought about drugs looking like anything other than drugs." He looked around the room filled with marijuana plants. "I'm never taking candy from strangers again!"

Detective Lawrence laughed. "That's a good idea. In fact, you should never take anything from someone you don't know. These days, you just never know what someone is up to. It's sad that we have to be so suspicious of people and their motives, but I'm afraid that's the way it is. I hope you kids don't forget that."

"I certainly won't," I replied, trying to figure out why someone would not only want to do drugs but to sell them to others too. I guess the Bible put it best: "the love of money is the root of all evil."

Even after a thorough search of the basement, exploring every nook and cranny, there was no sign that Mr. Baker had ever been there. The forensics[23] team had arrived and was busy going from room to room dusting for fingerprints and examining hair and skin samples. But from the looks of it, my uneasy feelings about Mr. Baker's being here were just that—feelings.

Once again, there was no evidence and no clues. While I was excited to have had a part in a drug bust which resulted in the arrest of two drug dealers—the same two druggies who had been on the trail that day—I was discouraged that we hadn't found any evidence to back up my theory that Mr. Baker had been kidnapped. As far as that mystery was concerned, it looked like we were back to square one. Our only hope was to explore the remainder of the trails and pray that we found some trace of Maria's missing father. Beyond that, I didn't know what else to do. For the first time since we had arrived in Delaware, I felt homesick.

Meanwhile. . .

As much as he hated to admit it, he missed the dripping sound. No, that wasn't exactly true. It wasn't the sound that he missed but rather the water that created the sound. It had been days since the water dried up. He licked his parched lips as he thought back to his last drink. The water hadn't been terribly cool or clean, but he hadn't cared. It was wet and refreshing to his dry throat. Without water, he feared he wouldn't last much longer, yet he knew he had to survive. Someway, somehow, he had to make it out . . . for Maria. She needed him, and truth be told, he needed her. "Oh, please, God, send some help," he whispered.

Chapter Nine:
A Stroll Through History

Back at Maria's house, the three of us kids sat on the couch while Mr. Solomon puttered about in the kitchen. Watson paced around Mr. Solomon, obviously hoping to catch some scraps of dropped food. From the quiet in the air and the somber expression on our faces, one might have thought we had just returned from a funeral rather than a drug bust. Disappointment hung in the air like a heavy smoke, nearly choking the life from me.

"I'm sorry we didn't find your father, Maria," I croaked, trying to fight back the tears of frustration.

"I know," she sighed as she allowed her tears to flow freely. "Me too."

Jamie said nothing. He sat hunched, his hands folded in his lap, smacking his feet together repeatedly. Even Watson seemed to feel the gloom as he lay on the floor, looking up at us with sad eyes.

We spent the next several moments in silence, then finally, I jumped up from the couch and walked over to the kitchen where Mr. Solomon worked on lunch. At my approach, he looked up.

"Mr. Solomon, may I ask a favor of you?"

He smiled. "Let me guess. You'd like to go back and finish exploring the trails, right?"

His question startled me. "Well, actually, we would, but I think we'd like to spend a couple of days back at Pop-Pop's. Don't get me wrong—we've enjoyed staying here. It's just that I don't even know where to go from here, and all the excitement of the past few days has left me exhausted. Maybe a couple of days of rest will help to clear my mind. Then we can explore the trails again, if that's okay with you."

After placing a pan of biscuits in the oven, Mr. Solomon straightened and looked me in the eye. "I understand completely, Abby. You've been through a lot the last couple of days. We all have. How about we eat some lunch, and then I'll drive you both home?"

I smiled. "Thank you, sir. I hope it won't be too much trouble."

"No trouble at all," Mr. Solomon said, "but I will need to chat with your grandfather about your sneaking out last night. I think he needs to know the danger you put yourself in."

"Yes, sir," I mumbled. "I was planning to tell him, but it might be better coming from you."

It was nearly two o'clock by the time we reached Pop-Pop's house, but he was still at work. Mr. Solomon helped us to get settled in the house and promised to call that evening to speak with Pop-Pop. After ensuring we were okay and making us promise that we wouldn't do anything dangerous, he and Maria drove off.

Watson hurriedly made his way to the living room and crawled up into his favorite chair. Within minutes he was asleep. If only I could have done the same, but I couldn't seem to shake the sadness and frustration that was eating away at me. Jamie, it seemed, was having a similar problem.

"What do you want to do until Pop-Pop comes home?" I asked.

He shrugged. "I don't know."

"We could take a walk," I suggested, trying to lighten the mood.

"Nah," he sighed as he plopped down on the couch. "I'm tired of walking."

I sank into the recliner and thought back over the morning's events. I wondered what the headline in tomorrow's newspaper would read. Would it mention the Delaware Detectives? Detectives, bah! Some detectives we were. We couldn't even find one man.

Realizing the downward spiral of my thoughts, I turned my mind to prayer. "Lord, I'm so discouraged. I really thought we would find Maria's dad today. One way or another, I thought we would be able to solve this case, but now it seems impossible. Please, help us, Lord. Help us to find Mr. Baker and to not grow discouraged." Before I realized what was happening, I dozed off.

"Abby, wake up," a voice said as something tugged on my shoulder.

"Hmm, what?" I asked, struggling to open my eyes. When things finally came into focus, I recognized Pop-Pop standing over me.

"Pop-Pop, you're home!" I declared. "How long have I been asleep? Is it that late?" I looked around the living room and noticed that Jamie and Watson were exactly where they had been when I closed my eyes and were both snoring soundly.

Pop-Pop seemed amused by my question. "No, it's not late. It's just a little after four. I came home early today."

"Oh," I said, straightening in the recliner. "How come?"

"Mr. Solomon called me at the store," he answered. "He told me what happened with the drug bust."

"Oh," I said in a small voice, looking down to avoid Pop-Pop's gaze. "I guess we're in a lot of trouble, huh?"

"You should be," Pop-Pop said in a gentle voice. "You're old enough to know better than to pull a stunt like that."

I braced for the rest of the lecture and the sentence of punishment that was sure to follow. But it never came.

"But from what I understand, you've already been lectured by both Mr. Solomon and the police officer. I don't know what I could say that the two of them haven't already said, and I'm hopeful that you're mature enough to have learned your lesson."

I nodded. "I have, Pop-Pop. I promise I'll never do anything like that again. I don't know what I was thinking." The tears I had been holding back all day finally burst forth like giant waterfalls. "I told myself it was the right thing to do, but deep down, I knew it wasn't. I knew it was dangerous, but I let my pride get in the way."

Pop-Pop handed me a tissue and patted my knee. "Yes, pride will do that. That's what makes it so dangerous. It lies to us and convinces us that wrong is right, even when we know better. That's why the Bible warns us about pride. It can cause a lot of problems if we allow it to."

"I see that now," I whimpered. "I'll be more careful in the future. I've learned my lesson. From now on, I'm going to stop and think before I act."

"That sounds like a wonderful idea." Pop-Pop smiled, handing me another tissue. "You should know that Mr. Solomon didn't call me at work to tell me about your little escapade. He was actually worried about you. He knew how upset you both were and suggested that maybe you could use something to take your mind off detective work for a little while. That's why I took off early. I figured we could do something together."

"What did you have in mind?" I asked.

His eyes sparkled. "Well, since you love history so much, I thought you might enjoy a visit to the history museum. I haven't been in ages, but they used to have some very interesting stuff there."

I gestured toward my brother. "What about Jamie? He's more into science than history. In fact, he thinks history is dumb and boring. I don't want him to be upset."

"I don't think he'll mind at all," Pop-Pop commented. "The museum has plenty to keep a young boy occupied. I think he'd love it. What do you say?"

Sniffing a final time and forcing a smile, I asked, "When do we leave?"

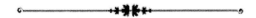

With discouragement still weighing heavily on my shoulders, I feared that even a stroll through history wouldn't take my mind off my troubles. But as soon as we entered the museum, I was overwhelmed with excitement and anticipation. Just a quick glance around told me that there was enough cool stuff to keep me busy for hours. I only hoped Jamie didn't grow bored before then. I needn't have worried.

"Cool, look at that over there!" Jamie said, pointing at a display of military uniforms and rifles. "Can we look at that?"

"We'll see as much as we," Pop-Pop responded. "Just remember we can't stay too long because we left Watson locked in the laundry room, but he should be fine for a few hours." Clapping his hands together, Pop-Pop seemed nearly as excited as I felt. "Where do you kids want to start, or would you like to wander around on your own?"

"Let's go look at those guns!" Jamie shouted, pulling Pop-Pop in the direction of the display that had first caught his attention.

"Is that okay with you, Abby?" Pop-Pop asked.

"Actually, I'm not really into guns. Do you mind if I look around on my own?"

Pop-Pop smiled as Jamie continued to tug him toward the rifle display. "That's fine. Just be careful and don't wander off too far."

"Okay," I replied, thankful for the freedom to look at the things that interested me like the old Indian relics and the chair that once belonged to George Washington.

As I browsed through the museum, I felt as if I were floating through a dream. I was surrounded by history and loving every minute of it. As I gazed upon the ceramic clocks, the colonial clothing and the tattered Revolutionary War flag, I forgot all about the morning's frustrations. My mind no longer focused on the drug bust or the disappointment at not finding Maria's father. Instead, it bubbled with questions about each artifact and exhibit. *What is this? What does it do? What was it used for? When was it used? Who used it?* While the questions were endless, I felt no frustration. Only curiosity and joy. In that moment, I couldn't understand how anyone could not like history.

Being a weekday, there weren't many people at the museum. A few tagged along behind a tour guide who stopped at each of the exhibits and explained their origin[24]. At one point, I thought about joining them but felt that I could probably see the exhibits better on my own. Anytime the tour group moved near, I walked on to the next section.

I was just about to do that very thing again when I caught hold of something the tour guide said. I wasn't even aware that I had heard her, but a single word echoed around inside my head, and I was pretty sure I hadn't read it on any of the exhibit cards.

"I'm sorry," I blurted out, coming up to the crowd from the side, "could you repeat that?"

The guide seemed a little upset with the interruption, but she responded kindly, "I said they used the cave as a shelter when they were on long fishing or hunting trips." She turned back to the crowd. "Now, as I was saying. . ."

The wheels in my head were turning, but I couldn't make sense of what I'd just heard. Unfortunately, I hadn't been paying attention to the first part of the tour.

"Excuse me," I interrupted again, "what cave are you talking about?"

This time, the entire crowd looked angry, and I was sorry I had asked the question. I could feel the heat rising up my neck and into my face and ears as the group stared at me. "I'm sorry," I said again, "I missed the first part of the tour, but I'm really interested in what you're talking about. Would you mind giving me a quick review? After that, I promise I'll be quiet."

The guide looked at the group before her then back at me. She took a deep breath, then replaced the smile that had disappeared for a moment. "Of course. We had just begun discussing the Lenni Lenape Indians. The Lenape were one of the first Indian tribes to come in contact with the Europeans back in the early 1600s. They lived in wigwams and longhouses and often fished in the nearby Brandywine Creek. During these trips, they would often stop to rest or take shelter in the Beaver Valley Cave, Delaware's only cave. I was just about to explain more about the Indian culture and show some of the exhibits which contain artifacts from their history. Does that catch you up enough to follow along?"

I hesitated. "Just one more quick question."

Someone in the crowd sighed aloud, but the guide only nodded at me.

"Where is this cave? Is it close?"

"The cave lies right at the state line between Delaware and Pennsylvania. It's about twenty minutes or so from here. We have maps available in the gift shop. If you'll purchase one after the tour, I'm sure we can find someone who can point out exactly where the cave is."

"Thank you," I replied in breathless anticipation. For a moment, I was uncertain what to do.

After butting in on the tour, I hated to walk off before it was finished, but as much as I would have loved to hear more about the Indians, what I was really interested in was that Beaver Valley Cave the guide mentioned. If I was right, the cave was somewhere in the area where Mr. Baker went missing. The trails that we explored the other day with Maria and Mr. Solomon were very close to the Pennsylvania border. But I had no idea there was a cave nearby. I thought there had to be mountains in order to have a cave. Delaware had no mountains. A few hills, sure, but no mountains.

I had no doubt, though, that if anyone knew of the cave, Mr. Baker did. Was it possible he took shelter there from the storm just as the Lenape Indians had? If so, was it also possible that no one thought to look for him there? I needed to find out more about that cave, but first, I felt I owed it to the tour guide (not to mention the group of people following her) to finish the tour.

Not that I was paying attention any longer. Nope, my mind was once again in full detective mode. Beaver Valley Cave. Could it be?

Chapter Ten:
Who Would Have Thought?

By the time the tour had ended, I felt like I was about to vibrate out of my skin. My fingers twitched. My heart pounded. And my thoughts, well, let's just say there was a tornado going on inside my head.

As soon as the tour group was dismissed, I hurried off to find Pop-Pop and Jamie. Thankfully, it didn't take long.

"Did you know Delaware has a cave?" I asked Pop-Pop as soon as he was within hearing distance.

Pop-Pop blinked. "A cave? Well, yes, I seem to remember hearing about a small cave somewhere around here. From what I've heard, it's not much—probably nothing like the caves you're used to. Why?"

Instead of answering, my mind raced to another question. "Have you ever been there? Do you know where it is?"

My excitement captured Jamie's attention, causing him to turn away from the exhibit he had been studying.

"What's up, Abby?" he asked.

"Yes," Pop-Pop joined in, "what's this all about?"

I took a deep breath and tried to decide where to begin my explanation. Once I had the words outlined in my head, I took another deep breath and let the words fly. "There's a cave in Delaware. It's actually right on the Delaware/Pennsylvania state line—very close to where we think Mr. Baker disappeared. Mr. Solomon evidently didn't know about it because he told us there weren't any caves around here, remember?"

Jamie nodded, but before he could speak, I continued.

"I think it's possible that Mr. Baker could be in the cave. Maybe that's where he took shelter from the storm. And maybe the police didn't check there because they didn't think of it either. The tour guide said that not many people know about the cave, even the locals. I think we should check it out. Pop-Pop, do you know where the cave is?"

Pop-Pop sat thoughtful for a moment then shook his head. "No, Abby. I have heard of the cave, but I must admit, I've never seen it, not even in pictures. Didn't the tour guide know where it was?"

"She said I could buy a map in the gift shop and see if someone could show us the exact location."

Pop-Pop rose from the bench. "Well, then that seems to be the first order of business. Are you kids ready to go, or would you like to look around a little more?"

"We're ready!" Jamie and I both shouted.

After making our way to the gift shop, we purchased a map and found another tour guide who knew the location of the cave. She placed a large red "X" over the area where we would find the cave. According to her, there was a small parking area just down the road from the cave's entrance. We thanked her for her time and the information and hurried out to the truck.

"Let's check out that cave," Jamie cheered as we settled in the truck.

Pop-Pop paused, then turned to look at us. "Now, wait just a minute. We need to get a little more information before we just take off. It would be wise for us to have a few facts first."

"Like what?" I asked, not understanding what other information we could possibly need other than the cave's location—which we had!

"Well, it seems I remember hearing that Beaver Valley Cave is located on private property. We can't go trampling around on someone else's land. Besides that, we might know where the cave is, but do we know how to get to it? Will we need any kind of gear? Does it involve going through the woods, and if so, for how long? There are many questions that need to be answered before taking off."

Pop-Pop's volume had risen as he spoke, but finally, he resumed his normal tone. "You kids are very good detectives, and you've done some great work. But one thing you're going to have to learn is to think before you act. How many times must I remind you? Always think things through. Get the facts. Assess the danger. Then, and only then, should you act. Do you understand?"

Jamie and I nodded, and Pop-Pop grinned.

"Good. Now, let's go home and make a few phone calls. Let's see if we can't find the answers to some of those questions. If all goes well, we can visit the cave first thing tomorrow morning."

Sitting back in my seat, I chewed on Pop-Pop's words. He was right. I had a bad habit of doing things before I thought them through. I guess I was just impatient. But the thought of waiting until tomorrow to check out the cave seemed like more than I could handle. As we drove home, I prepared myself for what was certain to be the longest night of my life.

We spent the rest of the evening learning everything we could about Beaver Valley Cave, which was not much, actually. After dinner, Pop-Pop dropped us kids off at the library to do some web searching while he drove back to the house and made some phone calls.

After an hour or so of digging and researching, we still hadn't found anything. Thankfully, when Pop-Pop came to pick us up, he told us that his phone calls had paid off, and he had found our little gold nugget— a guy who worked for a campaign[25] to save the valley in which the cave is located. Evidently, the township was exploring the possibility of developing Beaver Valley, turning it into shopping malls and housing complexes. There were a lot of people against the plan because the land and history that currently existed in Beaver Valley would be destroyed. Several of those people had gotten together and formed a campaign called Save the Valley.

Pop-Pop had spoken to a man named Jason, and he claimed to know the cave and the surrounding area like the back of his hand. He even offered to meet us the next morning and take us to the cave. According to his description, the cave was very close to the road, meaning we would be able to get to it easily and in a short amount of time. We wouldn't need any special gear or anything like that.

Jason gave Pop-Pop directions to the small parking lot the tour guide at the museum had mentioned and agreed to meet us at the parking lot at nine o'clock the following morning. With no other leads or offers for help, we eagerly accepted his invitation.

Even though we had spent the better part of the evening chasing down information, it seemed like night would never come. Part of me wanted to go to bed, thinking that the sooner I went to bed, the sooner I would go to sleep and the sooner morning would arrive. But part of me was afraid that I was facing another sleepless night and lying in bed waiting for morning to come was just no fun.

Pop-Pop allowed us to stay up a little later than usual, and the three of us enjoyed a movie that we watched using Pop-Pop's old VHS player. (Do they still make those things?) Watson, as usual, slept and snored the whole time.

After the movie, Pop-Pop ushered us off to bed, urging us to get a good night's sleep. I tried, really, I did, but once again, sleep just would not come. Thoughts rolled around and around in my head like clothes tumbling in the dryer. What would we find when we reached the cave? What if all this was just my imagination getting the best of me? What if our guide didn't show up? Aaauuggghhh, the questions!

When morning finally arrived, I surprised myself by jumping out of bed and rushing through the motions of getting ready for the day. With my clothes and shoes on, I made my way downstairs to the bathroom to comb my hair and brush my teeth. On my way out, I stopped by Jamie's bed and shook him as hard as I could.

"Wake up, Jamie. We don't want to be late!"

Jamie grumbled as he pulled the covers over his face, and I was once again amazed at how easily my brother could sleep. After deciding he could have a few more minutes, I hurried to the bathroom.

An hour later, the three of us—along with our trusty and well-rested sidekick, Watson—were dressed, fed and in the truck on our way to the parking lot where we were scheduled to meet Jason, our guide for the day. My stomach couldn't seem to decide if it wanted to cramp or slosh. I knew it was excitement and maybe even a little bit of fear. After all we'd been through with the case, I knew better than to get my hopes up. We had been disappointed so many times. I didn't want that to happen again. But I couldn't help the growing anticipation. It grew inside me like some out-of-control plant, and I felt like I was going to explode.

Thankfully, the drive to the parking lot was not a long one. Within thirty minutes or so, we pulled into a small, dirt and gravel parking lot, if you could call it that. It seemed more like a driveway than a parking lot. A large, black truck was the only vehicle in sight—not that you could fit too many more vehicles in the little space—so I assumed it belonged to our guide. As we pulled to a stop, a man who looked to be in his late teens or early twenties got out of the driver's side of the truck and waved at us, closing his door behind him.

Opening the passenger door on Pop-Pop's truck, I turned back to grab my emergency bag and realized that, in my hurry and excitement, I had forgotten to bring it. I couldn't remember a time I had ever forgotten my emergency bag. It was like a part of me, and I felt lost without it.

"I forgot my bag," I cried.

"So," Jamie remarked, crawling over me to get out of the truck.

"I just like to have it," I said, "in case of an emergency."

Pop-Pop looked at me from where he stood on the opposite side of the truck. "Well, hopefully, there won't be any emergencies. I think we'll be fine. Let's go. We don't want to keep our guide waiting."

Looking up, I noticed the guide was talking to Jamie, who was once again trying to control Watson who seemed eager to explore his new surroundings. Pop-Pop was right. I didn't really need my bag. Besides, it certainly wasn't worth going all the way back to Pop-Pop's house to get it. Instead, I crawled out of the truck and closed the door.

"Hi, I'm Jason," the man said, extending his hand to Pop-Pop and then to me.

"Hello there," Pop-Pop replied. "I'm Ed Patterson, and these here are my grandchildren, Abby and Jamie."

Jason smiled.

"Thank you for taking the time to show us around," Pop-Pop continued. "It means more to these kids than I could possibly explain."

Jason's smile grew. "It's my pleasure. The cave is right down this way. The easiest way to get to it is to walk down the road a bit then turn off to the left. The cave is not far from the road, but in the summer, you can't see it because the trees and bushes grow up and block the view. I guess that's why so few people actually know about it. How'd you guys hear about it?"

"At the museum," I chimed in. "The tour guide mentioned it when she was talking about the Lenape Indians."

Jason nodded and headed off down the road, motioning for us to join him. "I see. I didn't know they mentioned the cave in the museum. That's interesting."

In less than a minute, we were turning left off the road and climbing up a small, but steep hill covered with vines and bushes. Try as I might, I could not spot a cave. But as soon as we had reached the top of the incline and cleared most of the bushes, I saw it. Pop-Pop was right, it wasn't a large cave at all, and from what I could see of it, it reminded me of Jabba the Hut from the *Star Wars* movies.

"Oh wow!" our guide exclaimed. "When did this happen?"

"When did what happen?" Jamie asked, handing me Watson's leash and taking off to walk beside Jason.

"The tree fell. That big tree shouldn't be there in the opening like that. It must have fallen during a storm or something."

"When was the last time you were out here?" I asked, the wheels in my head turning with this new information.

Jason turned back to look at me. "Well, it's probably been close to a month or more. We've been so busy with the campaign and everything that most of us spend our days in the office."

"So this happened after that, right?" Jamie asked, beating me to the very question I was about to ask.

"Must have," the guide said, turning back to stare at the tree and other debris that surrounded and half-blocked the cave entrance. "It certainly wasn't like this the last time I was out here."

"Did you hear that?" Pop-Pop asked, his head cocked in the direction of the cave.

Struggling to hold back Watson who was continuing to sniff at the ground, I, too, cocked my head to listen.

"Help me," came a weak voice, so soft and cracked that I wondered if I had imagined it.

With my attention on the voice, I unintentionally loosened my grip on Watson's leash. He took off toward the cave, nose to the ground, tail straight and rigid. Just as he disappeared behind the tree, he began to bark.

"Watson," Jamie cried, "what is it, boy?"

Pop-Pop, Jason and I hurried to catch up with Jamie who had followed after Watson. Ducking under limbs and climbing over various sticks and chunks of wood, we finally made it into the mouth of the cave.

Chapter Eleven:
Safe at Last

A man, who I could only assume was Mr. Baker, sat on the ground, pinned to the cave wall by an enormous limb. He was dirty and seemed a bit disoriented, but his eyes were open, and he appeared alert enough to realize we were present.

"Praise the Lord," he muttered, resting his head back against the wall.

As Watson strolled over and sniffed the man from head to toe, the rest of us stood there like statues. I, for one, couldn't seem to make my brain work in order to figure out what to do next.

"Should we try to get him free of that big branch?" Jamie asked.

Pop-Pop shook his head. "No, that could be dangerous. We don't know what kind of injuries he might have. The best thing to do is to keep him still and call for help."

"There's no cell signal out here, but I have a radio back in my truck," Jason chimed in. "I could call for an ambulance."

"Why don't you do that," Pop-Pop replied.

As Jason took off back through the bushes and trees toward the road, Pop-Pop moved closer to the man. Jamie and I followed his lead, and upon closer inspection, I could see that the man was wearing casual shorts, a light-colored shirt that clung to his body and low-cut hiking boots. A dirty backpack lay beside him.

"Are you Mr. Baker?" I asked, praying that we wouldn't be disappointed again.

"That's right," the man said in a hoarse voice. "Do I know you?"

I shook my head, but Pop-Pop spoke before I could do more.

"Mr. Baker, we have quite a story to tell you, but in short, your daughter, Maria, sought out my grandchildren to find you."

Mr. Baker smiled a weak smile. "It looks like they succeeded." His expression turned to one of concern. "Where is Maria? Is she okay?"

"She's fine," Jamie said, grabbing hold of Watson's leash and pulling the dog away from the wounded man. "She's at your house with Mr. Solomon."

"Max?" Mr. Baker asked. "What's he doing here?"

Pop-Pop patted Mr. Baker on the arm. "As I said, it's a very long story and one for another time. Right now, it may be best for you to save your strength. It seems you've been through a lot. Can we get you anything while we wait for the paramedics?"

Mr. Baker ran his tongue across his cracked lips. "Water," he whispered. "I ran out a couple of days ago."

Pop-Pop turned to me. "Abby, oh never mind, I forgot you don't have your bag with you."

Immediately, I, once again, regretted not having remembered to grab my emergency bag. I always kept bottles of water in it. Pop-Pop knew that, but because I had forgotten the bag, this poor man was going to have to stay thirsty. Fortunately, my argument with myself was brought short when Jason returned.

"Help is on the way," he said, making his way around the fallen branches. "And I brought some water. I thought he might need it." He gestured to Mr. Baker.

Pop-Pop took the bottle Jason handed him and helped Mr. Baker to take a sip. After several drinks, he placed his head once again against the cave wall and closed his eyes.

"Thank you," he muttered.

Sirens sounded in the distance and grew closer. Within moments, a team of paramedics were climbing over debris and hurrying to check out Mr. Baker. After the lead paramedic determined that it was safe to move the injured man, he and his crew, aided by Pop-Pop and Jason, worked to lift the large branch off Mr. Baker's left leg and shoulder. Once free of the limb, he was lifted onto a covered board and carried out to the ambulance that had parked on the road just at the base of the steep hill.

During the process, Jamie and I did our best to stay out of the way and to keep Watson as calm as possible. Standing outside the entrance of the cave, we watched the commotion with both excitement and fear. We were happy and relieved to have finally found Maria's father. We were worried, however, about his condition. Would he recover? How bad were his injuries? I tried to listen in as the paramedics rushed back and forth, but they seemed to be speaking in some sort of code, and I really didn't understand much of what they said.

Jason stepped out of the cave and walked over to where we were standing. "Are you two okay?"

Jamie and I nodded.

"We're fine," I said, when a thought struck me from out of the blue. "Jason, you said you had a radio in your truck. That's how you called the paramedics, right?"

"Yeah, that's right," Jason answered.

"I was just wondering if we could use it to contact Maria. She's Mr. Baker's daughter, and she's been worried sick about her dad. Could we call her and let her know that we found him and that she can meet us at the hospital?"

"Absolutely," Jason smiled. "You'd better tell your grandfather where we're going so he doesn't worry."

Pop-Pop evidently heard part of our discussion because, at that very moment, he emerged from the cave and said, "Tell your grandfather what?"

Jamie spoke up before I could. "Jason's going to let us use his radio to call Maria and tell her to meet us at the hospital. Is that okay?"

"That's a good idea," Pop-Pop said, stopping to catch his breath, "but why don't we all go together? There's nothing else we can do here."

"This way," Jason said as he took off toward the road.

We had only walked a few steps when Pop-Pop stopped and looked back toward the cave entrance.

"Is something wrong?" I asked.

Pop-Pop shook his head. "I was just wondering if the police would be coming around to examine the scene. I mean, it's not like this was a crime or anything, so I don't know if they'll be coming out to take a look around or not."

"Who cares if they do?" Jamie commented.

Pop-Pop frowned at Jamie's tone. "It's just that Mr. Baker's backpack and other belongings are still in there. I was just wondering if we should take them with us so we can return them to Mr. Baker or, at least, Maria, at the hospital."

"That's probably not a bad idea," said Jason from several feet away where he had stopped after realizing we were no longer following him.

"I'll get it," Jamie said, already running toward the cave entrance.

"Be careful!" Pop-Pop called out after him.

Several moments later, Jamie stepped out through the cave's opening, hefting a pack that was nearly as large as he was.

"I don't know what all he's got in here," he said, "but it sure is heavy."

Jason jogged over and took the pack from Jamie. "Here, let me help."

"Thanks," Jamie said, massaging his shoulder and following right behind Jason.

Pop-Pop clasped my hand in his, and together, with Watson in tow, we made our way to Jason's vehicle where we made the call to Maria. After that, we climbed into Pop-Pop's truck and followed the ambulance and Jason to the hospital.

We had only been at the hospital for about fifteen minutes when Maria and her uncle burst through the glass doors.

"Where is he?" Maria cried. "Is he okay?"

Mr. Solomon placed a comforting hand on her shoulder and squeezed lightly. "Calm down, Maria. Everything's going to be fine."

Pop-Pop stood to speak with Mr. Solomon but made eye contact with Maria as well. "He's alive and was conscious when we found him, but that's all we know for now. The doctor is checking him out and said he'd be out to give us an update as soon as he knew the details himself."

While we waited for news from the doctor, Mr. Solomon filled out some of the paperwork that had to be done for Mr. Baker. Once again, I longed for my emergency bag. If I had remembered it, I could have pulled out a book to read or done something to take my mind off the waiting. I couldn't even imagine what Maria must have been feeling as she sat there twisting the hem of her shirt until it was stretched and wrinkled.

Finally, after nearly an hour, the doctor stepped into the waiting room calling out, "Baker? Is the Baker family here?"

The entire group of us stood and walked toward the doctor. In those few short steps, I tried to judge the expression on the doctor's face. Strangely, he seemed neither happy nor sad, so I had no idea what kind of news to expect.

"He's going to be fine," he said, directing his attention solely to the adults. "He has sustained some serious injuries: a dislocated shoulder and two broken ribs. Also, his left leg is broken in three places. He has a long road to recovery ahead of him, but barring any serious infection, he should make a full recovery."

I looked over at Maria who had tears streaming down her face and realized that my own face was wet. She smiled at me, and we both hugged, laughing through our tears. Pulling back, she looked at the doctor. "Can I see him?"

"I'll let you go back for a few minutes, but after that, he'll need to rest. He's in a lot of pain, so we've already got him on some pain medication. He may be a bit groggy, so make your visit quick."

The doctor turned and led us through the door and down the hallway to a small room on the right. Mr. Baker lay on a hospital bed, a tangle of wires stringing from his body to the machines surrounding him. He was covered with a blanket so his injuries couldn't really be seen, but there was no missing the leg that was wrapped completely in a cast and held in the air by some sort of sling hanging down from above the bed.

As soon as we entered the room, Maria rushed to the bed and wrapped her arms around her father as best she could. The rest of us stood at the back of the room, trying to give them the time they needed.

"I really should be going now," Jason whispered to Pop-Pop. "I just wanted to stay long enough to hear what the doc said, but I need to get back to work now."

Pop-Pop shook his hand. "We can't thank you enough, young man. As far as I'm concerned, you're a hero."

Jason smiled and shook his head. "Nah, not me, but these two," he pointed over at Jamie and me, "these two really are heroes. They're the ones who figured out where to look. I just led the way. That's all." He winked at us, then turned back to Pop-Pop. "You have some fine grandchildren. You should be proud of them."

Pop-Pop returned the smile. "Oh, believe me, I am."

Jason left the room, then immediately popped his head back through the doorway. "What do you want me to do with his backpack?"

"He could leave it in your truck," I suggested, "and we could get it to Maria or Mr. Baker later."

Pop-Pop nodded. "Yes, that would work. Do you mind just setting it in the truck, Jason? We parked right beside you. Oh, and be careful. Watson's in there too."

Jason smiled again. "I don't mind at all, sir." With that, he was gone.

When I looked back toward the bed, I noticed Mr. Baker was motioning for us to get closer. We shuffled to the bed and stood quietly.

"I just wanted to thank you all," Mr. Baker said in a tired, scratchy voice. "You saved my life, and I can never repay you."

"You don't have to repay us," Jamie spoke up. "We're just glad you're okay."

The injured man closed his eyes and smiled. "Still, I am eternally grateful. You are now friends for life!" His words were beginning to slur.

Mr. Solomon stepped a little closer. "Dan, the doctor says you need to get some rest, so we're going to leave you alone for now. We'll be back a little later, okay? Do you need anything?"

Mr. Baker closed his eyes again and shook his head. "Just my fish," he mumbled.

I looked over at Mr. Solomon, but he seemed to be just as confused as I was.

"I believe his medication is kicking in," Pop-Pop said. "We need to go now. Besides, we have a rambunctious puppy in the truck. We shouldn't keep him cooped up any longer."

As we turned to exit the room, Jamie whirled around and hurried back to Mr. Baker's bedside. Reaching in his pocket, he pulled out what appeared to be a knife. "I almost forgot, Mr. Baker, I think this must have fallen out of your backpack. It was on the ground beside where you were trapped."

Maria's dad struggled to open his eyes, then reached and grabbed the knife with his one good arm. He studied the object for a moment, shook his head and placed it back in Jamie's hand. "'Snot mine," he slurred[26].

"Are you sure?" Jamie asked, but Mr. Baker had fallen asleep.

Jamie returned the object to his pocket, and the three of us made our way back to Pop-Pop's house.

Chapter Twelve:
Lost and Found

As soon as we opened the door to Pop-Pop's house, Watson bolted into the house and jumped up into his favorite chair. In contrast to the dog's boundless energy, Pop-Pop limped over to the phone and began checking the messages.

I sat down on the couch until he was finished but jumped up as soon as he hung up the phone. "Pop-Pop, are you okay? You're limping."

He smiled. "I'm fine, sweetie. I'm just not as young as I used to be, and I'm afraid that little hike today was just a bit much for my tired, old bones. Nothing a good night's rest won't fix."

At the mention of rest, I suddenly felt extremely tired. My body ached. My head throbbed. And I felt like I could curl up on the couch and take a nap. I was about to ask Pop-Pop if he would mind when he spoke.

"Still no calls about the dog. If someone owns him, they don't seem to be looking for him very hard. You kids have posters all over town. You've notified the animal shelter. I thought for sure someone would have called by now."

I frowned and asked the question I had hoped would never have to be asked. "What do we do if no one claims him?"

"Can we keep him?" asked Jamie who entered the room and sat down on the arm of the chair Watson was curled up in.

Pop-Pop looked shocked. "Well, Jamie, I don't mind him staying here for a while, but you kids will be going home soon. I can't take care of him alone."

"He can come with us," Jamie insisted.

"To South Carolina?" I asked.

"Sure, why not?"

"That'll have to be up to your parents, Jamie. I'm not sure how they'll feel about having a dog."

"And I'm really not sure how they'll feel about taking a dog in the car for a twelve hour ride," I added.

Jamie patted Watson, who stuck out his enormous tongue and looked around playfully. "It won't hurt to ask," Jamie said.

Pop-Pop sighed. "Perhaps tomorrow. I think we've all had enough excitement for one day. I, for one, could use a nap. Will you kids be okay if I rest for a bit?"

"I was thinking about doing the same thing," I said.

Nodding, Pop-Pop said, "See you in a bit then." He limped off toward his bedroom.

I considered going to my bedroom as well, but my body didn't seem interested in moving. It was as if the couch had suddenly grown strong arms that were holding me captive in its embrace. Reaching for the nearest pillow, I shoved it under my head, settled myself more firmly into the couch cushions and closed my eyes.

"I wonder who this belongs to?" Jamie asked.

Opening my eyes, I saw that he was looking at a small wooden knife, turning it this way and that and scrunching his eyes and forehead as if trying to see something that wasn't there.

"What are you doing?" I mumbled.

He looked up at me. "It says something here on the handle, but it just looks like a bunch of letters. Maybe it's another language."

I snuggled deeper into the pillow and closed my eyes again. "Maybe. Or maybe it's Mr. Baker's. You heard him. He was out of his mind on those pain killers. He may not have realized what it was. You can ask him about it later."

I intended to say more, but my body wouldn't allow it. All the nights of stolen sleep finally caught up with me, and I found that I could no longer resist its call.

The next morning, Pop-Pop had to go back to work, even though he was still limping. Shortly after we awoke, Mr. Solomon called and offered to pick us up and take us to the hospital to visit with Maria and Mr. Baker. From what Maria's uncle told us, Mr. Baker was doing much better though he was still in some pain.

Jamie and I jumped at the opportunity to see Maria although we hated to have to lock Watson in the laundry room again. Still, there was no way they'd allow him into the hospital. After feeding him and giving him a few treats, I patted him on the head and promised to take him to the park when we got back. I don't know if he understood, but his ears perked up when I mentioned the park, so maybe he did. Who knows how much dogs really understand? I definitely think they're smarter than some people I know.

It turned out that Mr. Solomon's report was true. When we entered the hospital room, the first thing I noticed was that Mr. Baker was propped up in a seated position, though his leg still dangled from the sling. His face was clean, and his hair even appeared to be combed. To tell the truth, he didn't even look like the same man we had rescued the day before.

"There are my heroes!" he said as soon as he spotted us.

His voice, though still hoarse, was not slurred like it had been earlier.

For several minutes, we told Mr. Baker how Maria had asked us to find him and about the disappointments of not having any clues to go on. We filled him in about the drug operation in his neighborhood which, it turned out, he knew nothing about. Then we finished the tale with our trip to the museum and my idea that maybe he had taken shelter in the cave to wait out a storm.

"That's exactly what happened, young lady," Mr. Baker said. "I was doing my usual rounds on the trails when this huge storm came up out of nowhere. There were a couple of other shelters I could have chosen. There was even a big historic house near my position. But I remembered the stories I had heard over and over again about the Lenape Indians and how they took shelter in Beaver Valley Cave. I knew where the cave was and that it wasn't far. Unfortunately, I was standing too close to the entrance. I wanted to watch the storm without really being out in it, so I stood at the mouth of the cave and watched as the rain fell, the wind blew and the lightning flashed."

"Then what happened?" Jamie interrupted.

"Well, it happened so fast. One minute I was watching the storm, the next minute this huge tree came crashing down. As the limbs hit the top of the cave, several of them broke off. I guess maybe they ricocheted[27] off the tree itself. I'm not really sure. All I know is that they came bouncing toward me out of nowhere, and before I could get out of the way, they struck me and pinned me to the wall."

He shifted in the bed and grimaced at the obvious pain he suffered from the movement. Once he had caught his breath, he opened his eyes again. "I struggled for a while, but pretty soon, I realized that all I was doing was making things worse. For days, I cried out, hoping that someone would pass by close enough to hear me. But after a while, my voice was gone, and all I could do was sit there and pray that someone would find me before it was too late."

I swallowed hard to fight back the tears that were threatening to escape. "How did you survive? I mean, what did you eat and drink?"

Mr. Baker smiled. "Thankfully, I'm one of those hikers who believes in always being prepared for an emergency. I had a good supply of water and some protein bars in my pack. That got me by for a while, and when my water ran out, there was a small pool that formed nearby from the rain water that ran down from the upper part of the cave. It wasn't the cleanest water, but it was better than no water at all. Unfortunately, even that dried up a few days ago. That's when I really started to get scared."

"You survived all that time on protein bars and rain water?" Jamie asked.

Mr. Baker chuckled, then grimaced at the obvious pain the slight movement had caused. "Well, the first couple of days, I didn't eat anything. I sipped on the water in my pack, drinking just a little bit each hour. When my hunger got the best of me, I decided to ration out what food I had. I broke my protein bars into little pieces and ate one piece each hour along with my water. It certainly didn't satisfy my hunger, but since I wasn't exerting much energy, it was enough to keep me alive. I'm just glad I paid attention during those survival courses I took a while back. I never realized just how important that knowledge would be. It saved my life." Mr. Baker paused and looked toward the ceiling. "Well, that and a lot of prayer."

Before he could say more, a nurse entered the room. "I'm afraid you'll have to leave now. We have to run some tests on Mr. Baker, but you're welcome to come back later."

As Maria was saying her good-byes, Jamie once again reached into his pocket and pulled out the wooden knife.

"I think this is yours, Mr. Baker. I tried to give it to you last night, but you didn't seem to recognize it."

Mr. Baker took the knife and examined it closely. "Hmm, I'm afraid it's not mine. It looks quite old—like something from a museum. Why did you think it was mine?" He handed the knife back to Jamie who took it and rubbed his finger over the engraving.

"It was close to your pack when we found you yesterday. It was just lying there on the ground, like maybe you had dropped it. I just assumed it was yours."

Mr. Baker shook his head. "No, sorry. It's not mine."

"You really must go now," the nurse said in a less than pleasant tone.

Back at Pop-Pop's, I kept my promise to Watson, and Jamie and I took him on a walk to the park. While the energetic dog ran and played, I glided back and forth in the swing.

Jamie, being much quieter than usual, sat down on the ground beside the swing and pulled the knife out of his pocket once more. "I wish I knew who this belongs to.

"It probably belongs to someone who visited the cave, that's all," I said. "If you're really that upset about it, we can take it to the police so they can hold it in case anyone reports it missing."

Jamie rubbed his finger across the markings. "No, there's something special about this knife. Something—I don't know—mysterious."

"It's a knife," I said. "There's nothing mysterious about it."

Jamie looked up. "Then what about this strange writing, huh? That's *not* nothing."

I took the knife from his outstretched hand and studied the inscription. I wasn't ready to say that there was some sort of mystery surrounding the knife, but one thing was for sure—the inscription did look like a jumble of letters. Maybe Jamie was right. Maybe it was a different language.

"NATA SEKSIT TEME," I read aloud. "I have no idea what that means."

"Me neither," Jamie mumbled, dragging his hand through his hair and letting out a deep breath.

"Well then, dear brother, it looks like we have another mystery to solve."

"You mean it?" he asked, jumping to his feet.

I smiled. "Absolutely! After all, that's what we do."

Science Center

You may be wondering if Jamie's trick with the pirate patch really works. Actually, it does, though whether or not it is the real reason pirates wore a patch over one eye is not certain. The theory was tested on a Discovery Channel show called *Mythbusters,* where the hosts attempted to work their way through an obstacle course in the dark—first without using the eye patch method and then a second time after wearing an eye patch for approximately thirty minutes. The results were amazing. Not only did each of the hosts get through the course faster, but each of them did it without running into anything or making any mistakes. Each testified that he could see clearly after switching the patch from one eye to another as opposed to the first trip through the maze where everything was pitch black.

How does it work?

There are two parts at the back of the retina in your eye that are responsible for seeing. The cones see colors and details and work best in bright light. The rods deal more with black and white and work best in low-light situations. The thing is that when you move from light to dark, your cones (which have been actively working) can't see well, and your rods (which weren't needed in the light) take a while to warm up. In fact, scientists say that it can take nearly twenty-five minutes for our eyes to adjust completely to a dark room. By placing a patch over one eye, you're essentially telling the rods in that eye that they need to start working. If you allow them sufficient time to warm up then switch the patch to cover the eye in which the cones are actively working, you should be able to see just as clearly in the dark as you did in the light. Why don't you try it out and see how well it works?

History Hideout

The Lenni Lenape (pronounced Leh-nee Leh-nah-pay) Indians, also known as the Delaware Indians, were some of the first Indians to come in contact with the Europeans in the early 1600s. They lived in small groups in the "Land of the Lenape" which included what is now New Jersey, eastern Pennsylvania, southeastern New York, northern Delaware and a small portion of southeastern Connecticut. Unlike the many Western Plains Indians we think of, the Lenape did not live in teepees but rather in wigwams and longhouses. The men worked as hunters and farmers while the women took care of the children and the chores around home like cooking and cleaning and gardening. The Lenape *did* often seek refuge and shelter in Beaver Valley Cave. Since the cave was close to water, it provided the perfect stopping place for the Indian hunters to rest and eat when their hunts would take them far from home. Like most Indian cultures, the Lenape have a history of stories and legends that have been handed down over the generations. The Lenape Indians currently reside in Oklahoma, and most wear modern clothes, live in houses and drive cars.

There is a lot of information about the Lenni Lenape Indians on the web, so I encourage you to do some digging and see what you can discover about this interesting tribe. Here are a few sources to help you get started:

Lenape Indian Fact Sheet -
http://www.bigorrin.org/lenape_kids.htm
About the Lenapes -
http://www.lenapelifeways.org/lenape1.htm
Penn Treaty Museum -
http://www.penntreatymuseum.org/americans.php

If you'd like to find out a bit more about Beaver Valley Cave, you can check out these sites:

Commander Cody Caving Club -
http://www.caves.org/grotto/cccc/Cave_DE.html
Universal Skills -
http://universalskills.blogspot.com/2007/06/exploring-beaver-valley-rock-shelter.html

Glossary of Terms

1 illuminating – lighting up
2 rummaging – searching for something
3 cooed – talked in a soft, loving way
4 formulated – created; thought of
5 commotion – noise and confusion
6 theory – an idea
7 protested – disagreed with; disapproved of
8 indulge – to take pleasure in
9 freelancer – a person who works for himself, often finding various jobs in a related field of work (for example, writing)
10 ferocious – violent, extreme or fierce
11 menacing – threatening; angry
12 ill-kept – in poor condition; shabby
13 moderate – neither too much nor too little; in this case, not too fast or too slow
14 Mason-Dixon – a line dividing the Northern ans Southern states during the Civil War
15 rambunctious – full of energy; overly excited
16 regretful – sorry for
17 acclimated – adjusted to; adapted to
18 maneuvered – worked our way; managed
19 contraption – device or gadget
20 identify – to say who or what something is
21 imperative – important
22 premises – a building along with its land and other outbuildings
23 forensics – science of gathering and examining information, often to solve a crime
24 origin – the beginning or source of
25 campaign – a series of activities to bring about a particular result
26 slurred – spoke unclearly with words that ran together
27 ricocheted – bounced off at an angle

About the Author

Dana Rongione is a Christian author and speaker living in Greenville, SC with her husband, Jason, and her two spoiled dogs, Tippy and Mitchell.

For a living, she writes quality Christian books for audiences of all ages and speaks to women on a variety of inspirational and encouraging topics. For fun, Dana devours more books than she does chocolate (though not by much). She also enjoys hiking, playing the piano, and spending time with her family.

To find out more about Dana and her ministry, visit her website at www.DanaRongione.com.

Printed in Great Britain
by Amazon